PERFECTLY MISMATCHED

Make Me A Match

KAY LYONS

Kindred Spirits Publishing

PERFECTLY MISMATCHED

Victoria Valentine—V to her friends—exited the taxi that had transported her from Wilmington's airport to Carolina Cove, North Carolina, and gasped at the pain that shot through her leg as a result of standing.

"You okay, miss?" the driver asked.

She ground her teeth together and nodded, the setting sun nearly blinding her.

"I can carry your bag inside for you," the man offered from within the taxi.

V shook her head, sliding the duffle to her shoulder. "I'm good. Thanks." She'd already paid him and tipped him, too aware of the fact he'd spent a large portion of the drive staring in his rearview rather than the road in front of him.

"Well, you have a nice night. Maybe I'll see you around here later?"

She pretended she didn't hear the comment and shut the door, turning to face the boats in the marina beside Reels, her father's restaurant and bar.

The Victoria bobbed in its slip but the *Siren's* and *Mermaid's* slips were empty.

Was he gone? Or maybe his captains had taken them out for fishing charters? Those were normally day trips only, but every now and again, someone would make an offer Vic couldn't refuse, and he'd stay out however long they liked, weather permitting.

She should've called. She'd had plenty of time to do that between flights, but every time she'd pulled her phone from her bag, the texts and voicemail messages from her mother had her tossing the phone back into her purse again. Her mother meant well, and her concern was out of love, but V wasn't in the mood, especially after a day of traveling and the pain it had caused.

Inhaling, she took a step and groaned softly from the stabbing jab that shot up her leg. She should've spent the extra money and traveled first class, because being cramped in the economy airline seats before climbing into the backseat of the taxi had left her leg cramping hard.

She eyed an empty bench along the marina and hobbled her way over, seating herself long enough to do a quick, and hopefully discreet, massage. Once the pain had lessened to a lip-biting level, she stood and tried again.

This time she moved a little easier and clomped along the sidewalk, ignoring the pitying looks from the couple passing by because she was a twenty-eight-year-old woman walking like she was eighty-eight.

V ignored the handicapped ramp on the right of the building and chose instead to brave the three steps leading to the door on the right. Her physical therapy included walking up and down steps, and maybe that bit of normalcy would help the tight muscles? Before being released from rehab, she'd been able to move up and down the stairs without issue. Well, much.

No pain, no gain.

She swung the door wide and let it fall against her duffle bag as she gripped the railing and began the process. Sweat broke out on her upper lip and the base of her neck beneath her coat, but she made it inside and lifted her head, only to catch the quickly averted eyes of those watching her arrival, probably because it had taken so long for her to get inside after opening the door.

"Hi, can I help you?"

The young girl's voice was much too chipper for the mid-March night. "I'm looking for Vic D'Marco. Is he here?"

"Is he expecting you?"

"Tori? Is that you?"

She turned at the sound of her father's voice and the childhood nickname and wondered who was more shocked. Her father stood a few feet away, still tall at six-four but grayed and gaunt and not at all like the man she'd last seen just hours after her accident. The last six months hadn't been kind to him, either. "Hey."

Vic charged at her like a bull and swept her up in his arms, squeezed her so tightly she wondered if she'd ever breathe again.

"Ah, baby, I can't believe it. What are you *doing* here? Why didn't you call me? I would've picked you up at the airport. How are you?"

"I'm good," she said as he set her gently back on the floor.

"Do you have an Uber outside? Suitcases?"

She shook her head, and his thick eyebrows rose when he noted the single duffle that had fallen to the floor during the embrace.

"You're traveling light."

"Last-minute decision." The thing about dancers who

spent the majority of their time in leggings and workout gear was that they didn't take up much room.

Still, something apparently gave her transient state away; she could tell because of the way he looked at her. She shifted her gaze, taking in the restaurant. "The place looks great."

It was a dive. But it was a cute, beachy dive with painted signs and that quintessential beach vibe that drew tourists and locals alike.

The last time she'd seen the restaurant and bar was… what, six hurricanes ago? Eight? She'd totally lost count. Maybe because she'd been about fourteen at the time and on the mandatory summer break visit ruled by her parents' divorce judge. After that summer, she'd managed to snag prime spots with dance companies and spent every summer afterwards training, practicing, and performing.

"Made some changes over the years when I could. Come sit down. You're staying with me, right?"

"Um, yeah. If that's okay?"

She followed him to the corner of the long bar and took a stool, glad it allowed her to sit and rest yet still stretch her long legs.

"You know you always have a place with me."

He'd told her that a lot over the years. But this was the first time she'd ever been tempted—or forced—to make use of the offer.

Had anyone told her an injury could take on an identity of its own, she would've said they were crazy. Six months after the fact, she knew it to be true, and it only added to the losses she felt as a result of one wrong move.

"Ah, sweetheart, you look exhausted. How about I drive you to my place and come back to do what I need to do?"

"No. Don't be silly. I need to decompress a bit," she said, forcing a smile. "I can sit here as well as there."

"You're sure?"

"Yes."

He didn't look convinced but seemed to take her at her word, anyway.

"You hungry? Thirsty?"

"A glass of wine would be nice." Maybe it would take the edge off the pain, too. She was exhausted but wired and knew sleep would be elusive, at least for several hours yet.

Truthfully, she'd love nothing more than a walk on the beach in the dark where no one could see her limping along. Her father had always said saltwater healed everything, and right now she would love nothing more than for that to be true.

Vic stepped behind the bar and took a look through some bottles, finally finding one he approved of.

"Best we have."

"Don't open that just for me."

"Hey, it isn't every day my little girl comes to visit. We're celebrating."

He set to work on the cork, and seconds later, a freshly poured glass appeared in front of her. "Thanks."

"Still feels like I ought to be carding you. You look too young for that."

"Hardly. But thanks again."

Her father grabbed a bottle of water from the fridge and held it up to her.

V lifted her glass, wishing she had something to celebrate, and instead blinked back tears as she lightly tapped the bottle and fought to maintain her composure in her exhausted state.

"Baby girl, as thrilled as I am to see you, shouldn't you be in New York? In therapy? What are you doing here?"

She inhaled and squared her shoulders. "Before I got hurt, you mentioned you've had a hard time juggling the charters and the restaurant, so I thought maybe… I could help."

"Help? You want a job?"

"Why not?"

"So this isn't just a visit? You plan on staying in Carolina Cove?"

She took a sip of her wine and felt the intensity of his gaze. "Until I'm ready to get back to my company, yeah. If you agree, I mean. Can I stay?"

Chapter 2

MacGregor Jones excused himself from the group gathered around a patio table of the riverfront restaurant and answered the buzzing phone in his hand after spying the name. "Hello?"

"Hey, Mac. I hate to do this but I need a favor."

Mac frowned at the man's comment and quickly moved to a less noisy spot along the river walk. "What's going on?"

He'd been working a deal with the man for the last month to buy his business and hoped the call wasn't going to end the process and make the effort a waste of time.

"Something's come up and I need to reschedule our meeting," the guy clarified.

"Rescheduling isn't a problem. Next week?"

"Actually, no. Might be a few weeks. I need some time."

"How much time?" Mac asked, growing even more suspicious.

"I'm not sure. Can I let you know?"

Mac ran a hand over his head and leaned against the railing behind him. "If you're shopping around—"

"I'm not, man. You know my story and I know you're giving me a good deal. I just need time and headspace to deal with something important. That's all."

The man's words rang with truth, and considering Mac knew the guy had his hands full already, he wondered what else had happened. Another bad test result? He didn't want to pry and wasn't brave enough to ask. "Okay, yeah, that's fine. Do what you need to do and let me know when you're ready to move forward."

"Thanks. I appreciate it."

The phone clicked in his ear, and Mac tucked it away in a pocket, lingering inside the wooden alcove along the waterway due to the peacefulness it brought.

"Something wrong?" Marsali asked from behind him.

He turned to look at his sister, wondering if he'd ever seen her this happy. She and his best friend had gotten together just before Valentine's Day, and the two had been inseparable since. "No, just work. You and Oliver are house hunting, huh?"

"House hunting, wedding planning…" She took a deep breath. "It's a little overwhelming."

"But you're happy?"

A huge grin broke over her face.

"Words can't begin to describe it."

He tugged her toward him and gave her a one-armed hug. "Good. But if you ever need me to, I'll still give him a beatdown."

Marsali laughed and lightly punched his stomach. "He's your best friend."

"Best friend or not, he messed with my baby sister," he grumbled.

She leaned her curly head back on his arm and stared up at him, grinning from ear to ear. "Or maybe your baby sister messed with him."

Mac winced. "Yeah, I don't want to hear that."

A throaty chuckle left her, more evidence of her high spirits. Marsali had had a crush on Oliver for as long as Mac could remember, but he'd warned Oliver off, at first because of her tender age and then later because Oliver had chosen Hollywood over a normal life. Years later, Oliver had changed his mind, and the result was the ring sparkling on Marsali's finger.

"What's going on, Mac? You don't seem like yourself, and if I'm truthful, you haven't for a while."

He released her with a frown. "Nothing's going on."

"This is me, remember? I see it. I sense it. Are you really that bothered by me and Oliver making things official?"

Mac turned and lowered his arms to the top of the railing, shifting his gaze to stare out across the Cape Fear River. Two pelicans skimmed the water in the distance. "Nah. I think a part of me always knew it would happen." He shot her a teasing look. "You surprised me with the how, though," he said, referring to her very public blunder on national television when she'd outed her feelings for Oliver with an embarrassing slip of the tongue.

Marsali propped herself up beside him but faced the group seated outside the popular restaurant. Another round of laughter erupted, and he turned to look over his shoulder at the group consisting of his two neighbors and their new wives.

"There. That expression," she said. "*That's* what I'm talking about. What *is* that?"

Busted.

He lowered his chin to his chest and studied her much shorter frame. "Fine. You want to know what's wrong? I'm going to have to eat some crow, and I know it's not going to taste good."

"Oh? What happened?" she asked.

He took a fortifying breath and knew he wouldn't make it through without a lot of teasing and ribbing from his buddies—and their ladies, Marsali included. "Nothing is wrong. But here lately I've been thinking that… I'm tired of being the seventh wheel."

"The seventh… You mean with *us*?"

He watched shock roll over her features.

"Mac, please tell me we haven't made you feel unwelcome in any way."

Marsali was a sweet person. Too sweet in some ways because it made her more than a little naive and gullible. But she was always watching out for people and their feelings, checking on them, because she was such a caring person, too. She was good at reading people once she got them talking, something that helped her out a lot in her matchmaking business and the reason her dating guide had become a best-seller. "You haven't. But I think it's time you—"

"Don't you dare say you're not coming to dinner with us anymore. Or hanging out. Or… well, not doing stuff with us because we've paired up. I *mean* it!"

He chuckled at her fierceness, knowing it was born of love. "If you'd give me a chance to eat that crow I mentioned, I'd tell you I've changed my mind."

"Oh," she said, her tone filled with a little disgruntlement. "About?"

"You and"—was he really going to do this? Ready to do this?—"matchmaking."

The expression that crossed his sister's face would've been comical had it not been for the fact it was based on him placing himself and his future in her hands. As a big brother, that wasn't something easy to do on any level.

After all, he was the one who should be looking out for her, not the other way around.

"You mean…?"

He groaned inwardly. She was going to make him say it. "I mean I'm ready to throw in the towel and let you do your thing."

As a professional matchmaker with a ninety-two-percent success rate, if anyone could help him meet the right woman, she was it.

And after working nonstop to build his businesses and create a lifestyle he enjoyed, he found dating to be problematic due to the fact the women he found attractive, goal-driven, and yet family-oriented seemed to all be taken or otherwise involved.

So, if he was going to find someone to be eighth to his seventh, why not use Marsali's expertise to find a match?

"You're ready for me to *match* you?" she asked loudly, her green eyes flaring wide.

"Can we please keep this quiet? Otherwise the guys will never let me live it down."

Marsali practically jumped up and down in her excitement.

"I can't believe— Oh, my word! Yes! *Yes*, I can do this. I will find you *the* best—"

"Quietly?" he stressed.

She bit her lower lip and looked like she was going to explode from trying to contain her excitement.

"Okay, okay. I get it, but what about Mom and Dad?"

"They can't know, either. Who knows if it'll even work."

Marsali's insulted expression told him he'd gone too far.

"Excuse me, what did you just say?"

"You know what I mean. You're good at what you do,

but before we celebrate another successful match, let's actually find one, shall we?"

Disgruntlement scrunched her face before she nodded with a long-suffering sigh.

"Fine. I will say this—you won't be easy. But nothing worthwhile ever is. How soon can we do the interview?"

"I'm your brother. Do we have to—"

"Oooh, yes," she said, nodding. "The interview is even *more* important with you because I can't be your sister here. I need to know *specifics* on qualities you desire, pet peeves I don't know about, looks… you name it. And you have to be honest. *Brutally* so. You can't hold back with me."

"Okay, fine. Yeah, I get it. When do you want to do this?"

"Come by my house later tonight?"

"Tonight?"

"Yes, tonight. You've *finally* agreed to let me match you. I'm not taking any chances that you'll change your mind."

Chapter 3

Later that night, V lifted her gaze and looked around her father's new place. "When did you move?"

"Uh, not long ago," Vic said. "Only been here a few months."

"Can't say I looked forward to climbing the stairs to your third-floor condo. This is nice. I'm glad you chose one with an elevator this time."

"Yeah, me, too. Groceries were the worst."

She lowered herself into her father's recliner with an exhausted sigh and flipped up the leg rest and angled back, reveling in the surge of relief brought on by the change in position—until her gaze landed on some mail scattered across the top of the side table by her head.

What on earth?

Now that was a serious stack of bills. Radiology? Cardiology? Anesthesiology?

She stretched out a hand toward them only to have Vic swoop in and scoop them up.

"Sorry the place is such a mess."

"Dad, what is that?"

"Just some junk mail I haven't squared away."

"That's not junk mail. Those are medical bills. What's going on? Are you sick?" One of the dancers in her troupe had gotten sick two years ago. The kind of sick that required scans and radiology and—

"It's nothing, sweetheart."

Her gaze narrowed on his back where he now stood across the room shoving the literal handful of papers into a computer bag. "Dad, I can *read*. Why haven't you said anything? Does Mom know?"

"Your mother and I haven't been together for twenty-four years. There's no reason for her to know anything about my life."

"Okay, but what about me? Why haven't you said anything?" A thought formed and she groaned. "You've been sending *me* money to cover *my* medical bills when all along you've been going through whatever that is alone?"

"It's no big deal," Vic stated, turning to face her. "How about we get you settled and talk about this tomorrow?"

"How bad is it? *What* is it?"

He ran a hand over his thinning hair, and she studied him more closely than ever, realizing the bags and shadows under his eyes weren't only due to lack of sleep or too much alcohol but so much more.

"It… I had a heart attack a while back."

"*When?*"

Her father couldn't look more uncomfortable if he tried.

"A few days after I arrived in New York."

Wait, *what?* He'd flown to New York to see her in the hospital the day after her disastrous performance, even though he hated flying and everything about the city she'd called home for the last ten years. He'd been there after her first surgery, stayed a day or so, and then disappeared due to a… "That wasn't a work emergency. *That's* when you had it?"

A short nod was her answer.

"*Why* didn't you tell me?"

"Hon, I think you had enough to deal with without me adding to it."

"How bad was it?"

He grumbled under his breath and lifted a shoulder in a shrug.

"Bad enough. It required some surgeries and care."

Multiple surgeries? And yet he'd said *nothing*? "Dad, I'm so sorry. I wish I'd known. I should've been here for you."

"Baby, like I said, you were—are—dealing with enough. There wasn't anything you could have done to help me, especially not from the hospital bed you were in."

That much was true. But to not have known all this time… "What do the doctors say? What's your prognosis?"

Her father groaned and lowered himself onto the couch close to her, perched on the edge of the cushion with his hands clasped together in front of him.

"You're not going to give this up, are you?"

"Would you?"

He shook his head at her persistence and sighed.

"The, uh, surgeries repaired some things, but I'll have to have another one in the future. There was a lot of damage. Until then they said I need to eat better, exercise, and reduce stress."

"And are you?"

He laughed softly. "I'm a work in progress, just like you. Look, V, you don't need to worry about me."

She huffed at his statement. "Uh, yeah, I think I do."

"Everyone has something they're dealing with, right? Including you. But here we both sit, so it's all good."

All good? Not by a long shot. "I just wish you would've told me. I wish I'd known."

"You know now. So can we get to bed and get the rest the docs have told us both to get?"

A wry smile pulled at her lips. "I guess. Though right now I'd just as soon as sleep here."

"You've been keeping some secrets of your own, you know. You were limping awfully badly. Is it always that way?"

More often than she'd care to admit. She'd started training again while staying with her mother. She was a long way from being stage-ready, but she was very much a person who set her mind and made things happen, and admitting defeat wasn't an option. "It's from too much time spent shoved into cramped airline seats. I'll be good to go tomorrow and can pitch in at Reels."

"Now who needs to listen to her docs about resting?" he asked, standing. "Come on. You'll be more comfortable in a bed. Let me help you up."

"I can do it."

"Tori—"

"Dad, I've got it," she said, snapping out the words even though she told herself to dial it back. "I'm sorry, it's just… Please. Don't hover like Mom, or I'll go right back out the door and find somewhere else to crash."

He took a step back, hands raised in surrender.

"Guess now I know why you showed up out of the blue."

She fought back her frustration with herself, her circumstances, and those who meant the most to her. She knew they were trying to help. Everyone wanted to help. But she hated feeling like a charity case. "I'm sorry," she said, meaning it because pain made for lousy moods. "It's just... I know you know what the docs say, but I plan to prove them wrong."

"Tori—"

"And," she said, interrupting him before he could say what she knew he was going to say, "Mom was making it impossible to even breathe. All she could do was watch my every move and cry."

"Your mom loves you. She knows you're hurting. Knows what you've lost."

"*Temporarily lost*," she argued. "I'm not giving up."

"I understand, but before you come down hard on your mother, I've done my share of crying on your behalf, sweetheart. Parents tend to do that. Especially when we know our kid's dreams have been..."

He didn't say it but she knew exactly what he meant. And even though she recognized doubt in his expression, she still wasn't giving up.

Another huff left her as she grabbed the handle to the chair and flipped it and herself upright, barely managing to suppress the gasp of pain it caused.

Admitting defeat was *not* an option, she repeated to herself. A dancer didn't make it on Broadway without proving doubters wrong or, in this case, doctors, friends, *and* parents.

And if she couldn't? If she never made it back to the stage?

Then she'd go to Plan B. She'd accept her fate and adjust her thinking to accept the hand she'd been dealt. But until then? "I'm sorry. I'm just tired of the pity parties and I can't handle another one from you."

She didn't want them. Didn't need them.

Especially when she was *going* to dance again.

____

Chapter 4

____

Four days after her arrival, V mixed a couple of drinks behind the bar at Reels and found tiny umbrellas to add to the fruity concoctions. That done, she carefully made her way to the end of the long bar, the leg wrap she wore beneath her leggings and several days' rest enough to make drink delivery much easier.

When she'd first moved to New York City, she'd spent two years bartending and waitressing between auditions until she'd gotten her break and was actually paid to train and perform. The pay sucked and meant sharing a shoebox apartment with three other dancers, but dancing was life, and she'd lived her dream for eight glorious years.

And you will again. Soon.

She'd made a few calls earlier in the day to hunt down studios in the area but quickly learned there was only one on the island. She'd left a message but had yet to hear whether she could rent time to train.

For now, she was grateful for her bartending years, because they came back with every drink order placed.

"There you go. Enjoy," she said with a smile at the woman who'd requested them.

V paused when she noticed the woman hadn't stopped staring at her. "Is something wrong with the drink?"

"What? Oh, no, it's great," she said, even though she hadn't taken a sip. "I was just wondering…"

V waited, watched as the woman's unusual gaze narrowed even more.

"Are you single?"

A laugh huffed out of her chest. She hadn't been expecting *that* from the freckle-faced woman who looked like sugar wouldn't melt in her mouth. "Uh…"

"I'm a professional matchmaker," the woman said quickly, holding out her hand. "Marsali Jones of Marsali's Matches."

Marsali's Mat— "Wait, I've heard of you. Seen you on TV?"

The woman's cheeks flushed to a rosy color and brought out the coppery tone in her hair.

"Possibly. Probably," she then added, a wry twist to her lips.

Things began to click and V's brain filled in the blanks. She'd been in a rehabilitation center after her injury and surgeries when the entertainment news had gone wild with the story of how a childhood friend from North Carolina had snagged a Hollywood superstar. "*You're* engaged to Oliver Beck. Am I right?"

Marsali nodded. "That's me."

"Ahh, that explains the goon over there," she said, referring to the dangerous-looking man trying and failing to be discreet.

Marsali winced and wrinkled her nose. "Oliver insists on security until things calm down and people get used to us living here."

"Understandable. Well, nice to meet you, Marsali. I'm V."

"V?"

"Yup, just V," she said.

"Well, V, I hope you'll pardon my staring, but I'm *always* searching for clients or dates *for* my clients, and *you* would be perfect," Marsali said.

She stilled and raised an eyebrow high. "You don't even know me."

"Not yet. But you're beautiful, and I've been watching you interact with your customers. If you agree to be interviewed, I think you might be a great addition to my database, which is free. What do you say?"

As the woman finished her question, another slid onto the stool beside her.

"Do you ever stop trying to fix people up?"

Marsali slid V a wide smile.

"Job security—and fun. V, this is my best friend, Eliza. She's a magic-working wedding planner who is going to pull off a miracle for me and Oliver," Marsali said.

"Hi. V is short for…?" Eliza asked.

"Victoria Valentine," she said, using her stage name out of habit. She'd chosen Valentine since her birthday was on February fourteenth, and when she'd signed to dance professionally, her mentor had advised her to go with something catchier than her legal name. Now it was habit and currently kept her from being known as the owner's kid.

"Beautiful name," Eliza said, proving the mentor right yet again. "Is this mine?" she asked of the drink in front of her.

"Yes," Marsali said to her friend before turning back to face V. "Please consider it. Eliza is a success story. I found her a great guy."

"Yeah, he's tolerable," Eliza said with a grin, grabbing her drink and swirling the pink straw with a beautifully beringed left hand. "And for the record, I was totally resistant to her plans for setting me up but—"

"But love won out in the end, and she married the man I *would* have set her up with had he not taken matters into his own hands and gone after her himself after meeting her," Marsali said, lifting her glass to toast the statement.

"It doesn't hurt that he's really pretty to look at," Eliza added with a wink.

V grinned at the friendly banter that came from long-term friendship and shook her head. "Yeah, well, I'm flattered, but the timing isn't great for me. I'm not even sure how long I'll be in town. I'm… visiting."

"You're bartending," Marsali said, "so you *must* be staying for a while? Long enough to go out on a few fabulous dates with someone who might make you change your mind about leaving?"

A fabulous date sounded wonderful after the last six months of her life, but V lifted her shoulder in a shrug. "I don't know. An injury stalled my previous line of work, so I'm bartending until I can go back to it."

"What did you do before?" Eliza asked.

Tension filled her as it always did whenever she thought of her past. "I'm a dancer."

When Marsali's eyes flared a bit, V decided to have some fun. "Yeah, the pole broke and the roof caved in. It was a disaster. I barely made it out alive."

Eliza burst out laughing, and Marsali split her attention between the two of them, her eyes wide in shock and mouth opening and closing with no words emerging.

"Oh, Marse, come on, she's *teasing* you. She is *so* gullible sometimes," Eliza said to V.

Marsali's head shot back toward V, and she nodded,

smiling ruefully as she laughed. "I couldn't resist after I read your expression wondering *exactly* what kind of dancer I was," she said.

"Well, I admit I was curious. But not in a bad way. I don't believe I've ever met a dancer before."

"Yeah, well, I was a ballet dancer. I mean, I am but… injured," she said, shifting her gaze to the bar top so she couldn't see the pity that inevitably appeared. Why was this so hard? She was dancing. Training. Her career *wasn't* over.

"*That's* why you're so graceful," Marsali said.

Graceful? With a leg in a wrap that left her stiff and limping? She lifted her head and realized Marsali met her gaze with no signs of pity at all.

"You don't believe me? Even the way you mix drinks is graceful. I should've known you were some kind of performer. You have that lithe appearance *and* a sense of humor and beauty, too. All of which I'm looking for on behalf of my clients," Marsali added.

V took a step back from the onslaught of compliments and nodded to a new customer. The man took a seat several stools away and asked for a beer. "Thanks, but I'm not in the right mood to date at the moment."

"I'll get you in the mood," the man said. "You're new here. What's your name, sweetheart?" he asked when she set his beer in front of him.

"Bartender," V said, straight-faced, making it clear she wasn't interested given the undertones of his statement. Getting hit on as a bartender was certainly not a new thing, but some guys did it with way more finesse than others.

Thankfully the guy took the hint. He paid for his beer and took it with him to a table across the room, sending her a petulant glare in the process.

Did men really think comments like that were a turn-on for women?

"Sit down with me for an interview," Marsali said, lowering her voice so that only the three of them could hear, "and let me go over the process with you. If you *still* don't want to be part of my database, fine, but at least let me tell you about my business and how I do things before you turn me down."

V inhaled and leaned her hip against the counter to take the weight off of her leg. "My plan is to return to New York. I don't know how long I'll be here."

"Sometimes plans change," Marsali murmured, quickly explaining how she vetted her clients and even did background checks on them. "We're not talking losers out to play games. What's more, I have a VIP client who needs a very special match, and call it gut instinct, but I *know* you'd be a great date for him."

"Uh-oh," Eliza drawled, releasing her straw long enough to speak. "When she gets a hunch, she's usually right. Hate to say it, but you're doomed to participate."

Doomed? V laughed and placed both palms flat against the counter and stared at the women. They seemed fun, level-headed, and if ever there was an opportunity to get back into the dating world post-injury *and* breakup staring her in the face, maybe this was it? A nice evening out might take her mind off of the boatload of trouble plaguing her due to her father's health and the bills she'd seen before he'd hidden them. "Okay, fine. I'll do the inter-view and hear your pitch. But no promises about joining your database *or* dating."

Marsali and Eliza both grinned, and V felt the blast from across the bar because both women looked way too pleased at the news.

"You won't regret it," Marsali said.

V grabbed a rag and wiped down the already clean counter to give herself something to do.

The last thing she needed right now was another complication added to her complicated life.

Regret it?

She already did.

Chapter 5

Two weeks after his conversation with Marsali about being matched up, Mac reminded himself of Marsali's dating rules as he parked his SUV and made his way to the restaurant to meet his date for the evening.

Marsali had matched him up with a lady last week as well, but during the follow-up phone call, he'd told Marsali he was going to move on because he simply hadn't been interested. The woman had talked about her cat most of the time, referring to it as her baby, and then went on to bash her family. Neither trait appealed.

According to his sister, first dates were supposed to be casual. They were a chance to get a feel for chemistry and note any issues that could prove problematic.

The entire experience focused on knowing Marsali had vetted each of them and deemed them somewhat compatible on a surface level, so the next step was to figure out if there was enough interest and chemistry present to want to learn more.

According to Marsali, this date was "breathtaking" and

fun and possessed the humor and strength Marsali felt he needed in a match.

Mac made his way to the hostess stand and gave Marsali's name. The hostess grabbed a few menus and showed him to his requested table by the windows looking out at the Atlantic.

He sat down and ordered a drink, growing more nervous now that he was there.

Would she stand him up? Be beautiful but shallow?

The waiter brought his drink just as the hostess reappeared. He spotted a dark-haired woman walking behind the girl, but her face was obscured by the hostess's messy bun.

"Here you are. Enjoy," the hostess said, finally stepping out of the way.

Mac stood to greet his date and found himself sucking in air. Breathtaking was right. By looks alone, his sister had outdone herself. She was petite, a bare wisp of a thing that made him feel like a giant by comparison. "Hi, I'm Mac," he said.

"V," she said simply, holding out a hand.

He clasped her small palm in his, and she stared up at him with eyes such a light gray-blue they didn't look real. Contacts? "It's nice to meet you, V. You look beautiful."

"Thank you. You look nice as well," she said, lowering herself to her seat.

He'd stuck with business casual while she'd gone with a simple yet striking black sleeveless dress that wrapped her tiny frame like a second skin but remained classically elegant. She had good taste. That much was obvious.

Back in his own seat, he found himself trying not to stare like a teenage boy.

"Marsali—"

"Would—"

They both stopped speaking and stared across the table, smiling.

"You first," she said with a dip of her dark head and a direct stare from those amazing eyes.

"Would you like a drink?"

"Yes. Please."

The waiter returned with a lift of Mac's hand, and once she'd placed her order and the waiter disappeared, Mac found himself at a loss for words. She really was that beautiful. With sable hair and her unusual eyes, it felt like he was being sucked into a vortex. But he didn't mind. Chemistry-wise? He felt a definite match. "Tell me about yourself. Are you a native Carolinian? From Wilmington?"

She smiled at the questions, her hair swirling around her shoulders as she shook her head. "No. Far from it. I was born in Virginia—military dad—and lived there until my parents divorced when I was four. Then I moved with my mom back to her home state of New York and have been there ever since."

"You're a New Yorker?" he asked, unable to hide his surprise.

"Yes. And right now, you're probably wondering why Marsali set you up with someone from out of state rather than a local. I was, too, but… I discovered Marsali can be quite persistent when she wants something."

"Uh, yeah. That is an apt description of my sister." Marsali had been especially hard on him during the interview process, forcing him to home in on his preferences, attractions, everything. Based on what he'd said, he knew exactly why Marsali had chosen V as a match.

"Sister?" she asked, her eyebrows lifting in surprise.

"She didn't tell you?"

"No," V said, drawing out the word. "But that *does*

explain the VIP client comment she made. She insisted I wouldn't want to pass up a fabulous date with you."

The waiter returned carrying V's drink and gave them the dinner specials. V chose a grilled chicken salad and he ordered the crab-stuffed salmon.

"Fabulous, huh?" he asked, picking up the conversation where they'd left off.

"So far so good," she murmured, smiling.

He lifted his drink to her comment. "What does V stand for?" he asked before taking a sip.

Her red lips drew his gaze as she smiled.

"Victoria Valentine. And Mac is short for…?"

"MacGregor Jones." With their names officially shared, they stared at each other in a heady moment of awareness. Yeah, chemistry definitely wasn't an issue, but if she wasn't a local, why had Marsali set him up with her? "So you're… vacationing? Checking out the snowbird status?"

"Ah, not exactly. Long story short, I'm a professional dancer—ballet. I took a pretty epic tumble during a performance and am now on medical leave while I heal and begin training again."

"I see. So you'll be in town for a while?"

"Until I'm able to rejoin my company," she said, her gaze shifting from his while she slid a hand around her glass to lift it to her full lips.

"Do you have any idea when that'll be?" He didn't mean to pry, but he wasn't sure how he felt about a long-distance relationship. He didn't make it to New York very often.

"Um, no. Not at the moment."

Something about the way she said it made it clear her injury was a touchy subject.

"What about you? What do you do?"

"Nothing as exciting as a professional ballet dancer," he

said. "I'm in business, which basically means boring details and more meetings than I care to attend."

"But you like it?"

"Love it. There's something about the challenge of taking a business that's in trouble and failing and turning it around or realizing a need before anyone else and being able to provide it."

"You make it sound exciting," V said.

"It can be, for people like me."

"Here you go," the waiter said, returning with a tray bearing their plates.

They settled into eating and he liked watching her dig in. Despite her small size, she ate with gusto.

She took a bite as their gazes locked and she quickly chewed and swallowed.

"I guess I was hungrier than I thought."

"I like it. I hate it when women pretend they don't eat because they're on a date. But if you're still hungry, my dinner is great."

She shook her head and shot him a flirtatious look. "No, but thanks. I'm good."

He finished his meal and leaned his elbows on the table, hands clasped as he stared across the candlelight to where she sat. Even though she might not be in town long, he found himself hoping. Because right now he didn't want the night to end. "Dessert?"

Chapter 6

As a date, V wondered how it could be better. MacGregor Jones was tall, broad, and handsome with his dark brown hair and green eyes. He obviously spent his share of time in the gym given the muscles straining his jacket sleeves and the breadth of his shoulders, but he was intelligent and articulate and carried a conversation well, asking all the get-to-know-her questions typical of first dates while giving her plenty of time to ask her own.

Per Marsali's dating rules, he got the check and tipped well. Having spent quite a bit of time around her ex-boyfriend, Parker, and his stockbroker friends, she'd learned a lot about men from how they spent their money. Extravagant tips were usually about showing off and egos, cheap tips about greed. But those who were generous without being over-the-top? Those were the men who valued good service and were willing to recognize the people who gave it.

Those were her favorite, and she was pleased to note Mac was one those men as she took a discreet look when he signed the slip, adding enough to counter the waiter's loss of rotation when they held the table with their date.

"We've pretty much closed the place. Are you ready?"

She nodded and waited while he helped her with her chair and then walked in front of him toward the exit. That was nerve-racking, and she kept her steps slow and measured so as not to limp too badly. Sitting so long always left her leg stiff, but at the time, she hadn't paid any attention to the painful process due to the fun. She'd enjoyed the evening immensely and knew she'd have to relay that news to Marsali tomorrow, as well as whether or not she'd agree to a second date—if asked.

Once they were outside, Mac gave the valet his ticket while she took her phone from her purse to order a ride.

"You didn't drive?" Mac asked when he saw what she did.

"No. I don't own a car." And with her right leg injured, it would've been risky to get a rental or borrow her father's truck until she felt safe driving again.

"Let me take you home. Please," he added when she hesitated. "Marsali ran background checks, remember?"

"Even though you're her brother?" she asked, a little shocked.

"Yes," he said with a laugh. "But she did or I wouldn't be here now. Say yes." She stared into his green gaze and slipped her phone back into her purse. She wouldn't mind spending more time with him, and it definitely beat riding with a stranger. "Okay, yes. Thank you."

Within minutes, they were on their way back to Carolina Cove from Wrightsville Beach, and she stared out at the passing scenery. According to friends, it was still snowing in New York City, but on the way to the restaurant, she'd noticed things were already green and lush, the temp a moderately cool sixty-degree high with the low in the forties. Definitely something to appreciate.

"You're awfully quiet over there. Are you in pain? I, uh, noticed you limping a bit as we left the restaurant."

Oh, great. So much for her acting skills. "I'm fine."

"It's okay if you're not."

Seriously?

His comment earned a twist of her head, and she stared across the expanse of the luxurious SUV to where he sat behind the wheel.

Parker's thoughts and comments about the cane she'd used for the first few months and her injury and how it impacted his so-called image filled her head. Maybe Mac meant what he said. Or maybe it was just words? "I had to use a cane in the beginning. Or if I push too hard. Do too much," she said honestly. But mentioning her cane now? After a wonderful night? She figured it would be a good way of weeding him out of the future if he was the type to be bothered by such things.

Mac stretched a hand out to where her arm rested on the console, and he took her palm in his, squeezing her fingers.

"Bring it next time if you need to. Whatever you need to be comfortable."

"I'll look like an old woman," she told him, repeating Parker's words because they were so deeply ingrained in her mind. Parker had said he didn't have time to wait on her to keep up, catch up, or anything else. New York was New York, after all, and in the city, it was all about the hustle and bustle and perfection. A ballerina with a cane was not that.

Mac's husky chuckle filled the SUV, drawing her out of the spiral taking place in her mind.

"That's impossible," he said, lifting her hand to his lips. "In your hand, the only thing a cane would be is sexy."

Sexy? "Ah, I see."

"What do you see?"

"You have a thing for old women."

He burst out laughing and shot her a glance across the interior that nearly melted her insides.

"I don't know about that, but I seem to have developed a liking for brunettes with amazing eyes."

It began to sprinkle as they got closer to Carolina Cove. Mac had to release her hand to flip on the wipers, and she used the time to readjust the wrap around her bare shoulders and to give herself some distance.

Mac's charm proved to be a heady experience, and between the wine, her fatigue, and his easygoing rumbles of laughter, she found herself needing a bit of space. One date did not make a relationship, and seeing as how she wasn't even sure what her role in Carolina Cove was going to be… allowing things to happen too fast wouldn't be wise.

He crossed the bridge to Carolina Beach and kept going to Carolina Cove. She blinked to awareness and realized they'd settled into a comfortable silence she and Parker had never quite achieved. "That's it, up on the right."

"Nice place."

"My father's," she said as he rolled to a stop and put the vehicle in park.

"Stay put," Mac said as he left the SUV.

She gathered her purse and tightened her grip on her wrap, watching as he rounded the front of the vehicle and came to her side to open her door. He'd pulled beneath the drop-off area directly outside the building and now matched his steps to her much slower ones as she climbed the steps. Why did her leg have to cramp so much *now?* "You don't have to see me inside. This is fine," she told him outside the massive double doors.

Mac stood close, and she fussed with the edges of the wrap until he gently placed a hand beneath her chin and nudged her face up.

"I hate to see you in pain."

She closed her eyes and hated that it was so obvious. "I'm sorry," she said, unable to negate it. "I-I think I sat for too long and the weather… I'll be fine once I walk a bit."

"I hope so. I had a great time tonight, V," he said, angling his head.

"I did, too."

Mac hesitated before lowering his head, and she automatically lifted hers, welcoming the kiss he bussed over her cheek that left a trail of sizzling fire in its wake.

Her breath hitched in her throat, and her response to the old-fashioned gesture surprised her. Standing as close as they were, the scent of his cologne filled her head, pulled at her already dazzled senses, and left her shaky. His hands slid from her shoulders, beneath her hair, and up to cradle her head, his thumbs brushing along her jawline and heightening her awareness of him to the nth degree.

By the time he lifted his dark head—without the kiss she now craved—the world had disappeared, fading away with the light patter of rain on the roof above their heads.

One of his thumbs brushed over her lower lip as he stepped away, and she blinked to awareness when the cool, damp breeze hit her in the face.

Mac's stare, his touch. Her heart pounded in her chest in an adrenaline rush she'd only ever felt on stage. But considering it came from someone she'd only just met, it terrified her. A fun, fabulous date to pass the time while she was here was one thing, but when a man looked and talked and touched her like he had? Was this really something she was ready for?

"Someone wants to get out of the rain. I have to go but I'd like to see you again."

A car. A car had pulled up behind his SUV. Waiting. Silently pressuring them to speed things up.

For her to respond.

She bit her lower lip, and she watched as his gaze dropped and seemingly devoured before shifting to meet hers once more. That split second gave her just enough time to regroup and buy herself some time to think. "Thanks for dinner. Good night, Mac."

Chapter 7

The following day, V worked her first full day at Reels. *On St. Patrick's Day*, no less. All the while, her brain spun with her thoughts on Mac.

The evening had gone well. Dinner was delicious, her date handsome and intelligent, charming and articulate. But when Marsali had called earlier during V's break, she'd let the call go to voicemail because she wasn't sure what her response was going to be when it came to whether or not she wanted to see Mac again.

It was a fun date, a fantastic date, but why complicate her stay here with something that would end when she left? Especially when she needed to be focusing all her spare time and energy on physical therapy and dancing?

She poured another beer and slid it to a customer before grabbing a baggie from the stash she'd brought with her and moving to the ice maker.

Her friends would say to go with the flow of things, but she could tell Mac wasn't one of those men who'd be easily forgotten. And when her focus needed to be on proving the docs wrong, Mac was a lure that meant using time and energy on someone who couldn't become a priority.

V shoved her chaotic thoughts aside and filled the baggie halfway with ice before she grabbed a water bottle and left the bar.

She made her way across the interior of Reels toward the hallway leading to the kitchen and her father's private office.

Once inside, she felt her rigid body crumple a bit as she surged toward the desk. She rid herself of the extra items she carried and used the desktop to take some of her weight and pressure off of her leg as she collapsed into the worn office chair.

The leather smelled of Vic's cologne and the cigars he was undoubtedly forbidden to smoke, but she welcomed the comfort the scents brought as she lifted her throbbing leg to prop it up. She snagged the bag of ice and carefully placed it, sighing when the cold seeped through her leggings and offered blissful relief.

Her father had made it clear she could leave at any time since he'd only tagged her as an extra bartender to counter the craziness, but the St. Patrick's Day crowd had only just started to thin. She hated to abandon the regular bartenders on such a busy day—or not finish the shift she'd worked so hard to convince Vic she could handle.

According to him, she needed to rest, relax, and slowly increase her activity, not stand and work for eight hours straight on one of the busiest days of the year.

But who had time for that when she had to know one way or another if she was going to be able to go back to New York? To stay on her feet not only moving but dancing?

No offense to bartenders, but working a bar was a long way from training and dancing for hours on end, then performing on top of that. And if she couldn't handle a day like today…

She set a timer on her watch to alert her to the end of her break and closed her eyes, going into meditation mode in an attempt to lower her pain level. Meditation was something recommended by the therapist when she'd refused yet another round of pain meds. She'd seen more than her share of addiction over the years by dancers trying to stay in the game. And while the temptation was there because she wanted to dance *that* badly, she knew it had to be with a clear head. And if she couldn't return and perform without drugs…

Her lashes lifted as someone approached and a waitress hurried by. V stared out the open door across from her, unable to focus due to the noise filtering down the hallway.

Everyone was Irish on St. Pat's Day, but it was a good kind of fun as the chatter and laughter attested to. It wasn't long before yet another of the waitstaff hurried by. Yeah, meditation wasn't going to work with an open door.

She rolled her head along the back of the cushioned chair, spotting her water bottle on the other side of the desk where she'd set it. Thirst beckoned and she leaned forward, leg still propped and ice in place, and stretched out a hand to retrieve the bottle, watching in horror as it tipped to the side and the loosened cap went flying, dousing the papers beneath.

She gasped and scrambled upright, grabbing the towel still thankfully tucked at her waist to stem the flow just as a knock sounded at the door and someone hurried to her rescue.

She didn't bother lifting her head when a large male hand righted the water bottle and quickly snagged the towel from her to finish cleanup. She retrieved the splattered and dripping papers before they were soaked through and shook the water from them. "Thanks."

"You're welcome."

The words printed on the top paper jumped out at her about the same time as Mac's deep voice registered.

She frowned, still staring at the smeared letters of the purchase agreement. Wait, what?

She quickly scanned the page. Her father had actually *sold Siren Song* and *The Mermaid*?

She'd noticed them out of their slips again when she'd arrived that morning but thought it was because they'd been chartered and Vic's captains had taken them out.

"That should do it. And here's this," Mac said, straightening from where he'd bent to retrieve the fallen ice pack. "You should get that back on your leg."

"It's fine," she murmured, totally distracted by the news. "What are you doing here?" she asked Mac. "How'd you find me?"

"Well," he said, "I wasn't actually looking for you. You're just a really nice surprise."

Mac crossed his arms over his chest, and she couldn't help but notice the way his muscles bulged. He might be a businessman but he spent plenty of time lifting.

"Marsali mentioned that she hasn't been able to connect with you. She's waiting to hear your take on our date."

V faltered beneath the intensity of his stare, recognizing his interest because she felt it so much herself. "Yeah, it's been a crazy day."

She could've picked up, should have. But something had kept her from doing so. All last night, she'd stared up at the ceiling reciting the reasons dating Mac was a bad idea, but saying she wasn't interested would be a blatant lie.

His gaze shifted downward and then back to meet her gaze, a frown pulling his dark eyebrows low.

"You work here?"

Realizing he'd asked due to her Reels logo-ed T-shirt, she nodded. "The shirt says it, so it must be true. I thought I'd pitch in and help my dad."

"Your dad?"

She faltered at Mac's response. At the way his gaze sharpened on her even more and the tone he'd used. "Yeah. Do you know him? Vic D'Marco?"

"You said your name was Valentine?"

"Yeah. It's… a stage name. It's the one I'm most familiar with these days."

"Tori? You back here? Do you know if—" Vic broke off, spotting Mac. "Oh, hey, Mac. Nice to see you."

"Vic," Mac said with a nod of his head. "You've got quite the crowd out there."

"Yeah. We had a good turnout for the band," Vic said, his gaze shifting between the two of them to finally settle on Mac. "I see you've met Tori. Did you need something?"

Mac glanced at her at the nickname her father used. "V is my preference," she said with a shrug.

"You didn't mention your daughter was in town," Mac said to Vic.

"Yeah, Tori surprised me with a visit. What's that you have there, hon?"

Her father moved toward her, and V's fingers clenched the papers in her hands. He obviously knew what they were judging by the way he took hold of them while giving her a stern look. "You *sold* the charters?" she asked her father in a low tone, meddling even though she knew it wouldn't be well received.

"Two of them, yeah."

Mac shifted his weight and his big hands settled on his hips. "Vic, I'll come back later when we can talk."

"No, no, it's fine. Stick around. Tori needs to get back to the bar."

V stared up at her father as pieces began to fall into place in rapid succession. "Dad, why is Mac here to see you?"

Her father inhaled and exhaled roughly. "It's business." When she didn't blink or budge, he added,

"I'm making some changes."

"What kind of changes? Are you—" She broke off as Mac's comment during their date about buying businesses meshed with her father selling off the boats. "Did *you* buy the boats?" she asked Mac.

"No," Mac said, visibly uncomfortable with the obvious tension in the room.

"But you're buying something, aren't you?" she asked. "That's why you're here?"

Mac remained stoically silent, and after a moment, his gaze shifted from her to Vic. She gripped the edge of the desk not so much for support but to steady her stormy emotions as her stomach flip-flopped with unease.

Her father had owned Reels and the charters since her childhood, and something—some instinct—told her this had to do with the medical bills she'd seen on her first night here.

The problem? If her gut was right, it meant her Plan B was blowing up before her very eyes and the job she'd hoped to move into should Plan A not work meant—

"Dad, are you selling *The Victoria*?" The question was a last-ditch effort to salvage her backup plan and maintain hope, but the expression that flickered across Vic's face doused that spark.

Her father opened a lower desk drawer and shoved the

waterlogged purchase agreements on the two charters inside.

"How about you answer some questions," Vic said. "Like how you two seem to know each other?"

"We went out last night," Mac said bluntly. "But I didn't make the connection when she said her name was Victoria Valentine."

Vic's bushy gray eyebrows rose high on his wrinkled forehead.

"I see. How did that come about?" Vic asked her.

"His sister was in here one day last week," V said, "and she set it up."

"Ah, the matchmaker," Vic said, nodding. "I've seen her in here before. You didn't mention you'd gone out when I got home last night."

"Yeah, well, apparently there's *a lot* you haven't mentioned," she murmured dryly. "And all the stalling you're doing right now tells me there's more. What's going on? You just hired me to help with the bar and restaurant. Now I'm wondering why if you've sold the charters?"

"I still own *The Victoria*," he said a little defensively.

"But why sell the others?"

"I needed the cash, sweetheart."

"That much?"

Her father ran a hand over his head and shot a glance at Mac.

"Mac, would you excuse us?" she asked.

"No, I need to talk to him. Honey, it's fine. Mac knows what's going on," Vic said.

Great. So she was the only one who *didn't* know?

Vic inhaled and looked like a man with the weight of the world on his shoulders.

"Sweetheart, I wasn't well insured when I had the heart attack and surgeries, plus, I was out of state. Long story short, my insurance got picky about it, so they've only covered a small fraction of what they normally would have."

The air left her lungs in a rush. "Why didn't you *tell* me?" she muttered, hating herself and her injury because of the additional problems she'd caused. Because of the medical bills he'd paid *for her* because she didn't have the money, all the while being unable to pay his own.

"Because you didn't need to know."

"You're selling off your charters when you have a *charter business*. At least you still have *The Victoria*. You can focus on increasing her charters while I keep an eye on Reels and you get back on your feet."

Her father ran a hand over his head, all the way back to his neck, and squeezed so hard his neck turned white in the front.

"That's not gonna work, sweetheart."

"Because?"

"Tori, honey, I'm selling out to Mac. Things got sidelined when you showed up because I wanted to focus on you since you'd shown up out of the blue, but Mac and I already worked a deal. It's only a matter of making things official."

The news rolled over her, shook her to her core. Just when she'd thought she'd come up with a solid backup plan…

"Sweetheart, if you're worried about your job, I'm making it a condition of the sale," Vic said. "You're a great bartender, and Mac would do well to keep you on staff."

A condition of sale? Seriously? "What? Now I'm a charity case?" She shifted her gaze to find Mac watching her, his expression guarded yet decidedly uncomfortable.

The timer she'd set went off, and a huff bubbled out of

her chest, interrupting her father's attempts to soothe her upset.

She swiped her finger over her watch to silence the alarm and tried to steady her voice as she braved her response. "Look, Dad, it's okay. I only offered to bartend because I wanted to help you out."

"And you have, but you need a job."

"It's okay with me," Mac said, joining the conversation. "I don't have a problem with you staying on."

The air left her lungs. And even though she hated being a charity case, she *did* need the job, especially with the medical bills she had yet to pay. Staying on would save the time it would take to find something new. Even if she hated the idea. "My break's over. I have to go."

"Tori—"

"Can't have the new owner thinking I don't carry my weight." V gave them her best practiced smile before she turned and crossed into the hallway, blinking back exhausted, pain-riddled tears the moment the coast was clear to do so.

Plan B had been to come to Carolina Cove, help her dad and, *if* she needed to, start fresh if she couldn't dance. But that had just gone up in smoke, which meant Plan A—dancing—had to work. *Had to.*

She didn't want to be the charity case Mac had just taken on to appease her father and... she didn't have a freaking Plan C.

Chapter 8

Mac watched as V left the room, and he felt bad for the upset she'd tried and failed to hide.

"So Marsali set you up, huh?" Vic asked.

That was what the man wanted to discuss? "Yeah. She did."

"And?"

Taken aback by the man's question, Mac faltered. "Uh, we had a good time. I didn't know she was your daughter when I told Marsali I'd like to see V again. Or that she'd wind up an employee."

Vic waved a hand indicating Mac should take one of the seats opposite the desk and settled himself into the leather chair. "About that. I'm sorry to throw that at you the way I did, but I'm glad you agreed."

Mac sat down and stretched out his long legs, crossing his ankles. "She wasn't exactly receptive to the idea. Makes me wonder if she'll follow through, especially when she plans to go back to dancing."

Vic winced at Mac's statement.

"What?"

Vic's face got red and he sniffled, clearing his throat gruffly. "I love my daughter. She's smart and beautiful, but she's as stubborn as a mule."

"Wonder where she gets that from?" Mac murmured, smiling at the man's description.

"Mac, her professional dancing days are over. She just hasn't accepted it yet."

Mac's chest squeezed like it was in a vise grip. "What do you mean?"

"I mean, her career is over. The docs have told her again and again, but she says she's going to prove them wrong. Make a comeback." He shook his head. "It would be a God-given miracle if it happened."

The news sank in and Mac was barely able to breathe. Last night, when she'd talked about dancing, V had practically glowed from within, lighting up the room to the point she drew the attention of others in the restaurant as she talked. She loved dancing and it showed. "Doctors have been known to be wrong."

Vic pulled his phone from his pocket and tapped the screen a few times before handing it to Mac.

Mac pressed play on the video and saw V on stage in mid-performance, stunningly beautiful and dressed in costume, graceful and gorgeous as she flew across the stage with dizzying speed, leaping and twirling, practically weightless, faster and faster before leaping again—

He sucked in a sharp breath and sat forward in the chair when she landed wrong and tumbled across the hard floor, her cry of pain louder than the orchestra accompanying the show. But more telling than the fall was the fact she couldn't get up to get off stage. She sobbed, her face and body contorted in agony, curled into a ball with her leg cradled to her chest.

"I'd love nothing more than for her to prove everyone wrong, myself included, but she's got pins and screws and bolts holding her together in eleven different places from hip to foot. She still limps when she's on her feet too long," he said, his voice thick until he cleared it again. "My prayer is that she accepts what's happened and moves on. That she'll get to the point she can walk, run, exercise without pain. Beyond that?" He shook his head slowly back and forth, mouth pursed. "As much as I hate to say it, her returning to New York is the same as shooting for the stars. Slide over to the next picture."

Mac did as ordered, seeing an x-ray full of metal. He remained silent as he handed the phone back across the desk, wrecked by it all. The fact that she was on her feet after all of that was amazing and a testament to her determination and mindset.

"Tori came here because she wanted time and space away from her mother, but I think it's another way to run away from the truth finally starting to sink in."

Sometimes the truth was a bitter pill. "Facing that can't be easy."

"No. No, I don't imagine it is. She was one heck of a ballerina. The youngest to make prima in her company. An athlete in her prime." Vic rugged a hand over his face and inhaled. "Look, Mac, I know it's a lot to ask, but you've proven to me that you're a decent guy. So I'm asking. The truth will smack her in the face one day, and when it does, she's going to need something to focus on, whether it's a job… or a person. And something makes me think you're a little of both right now."

Mac frowned and shifted uncomfortably. "Vic, we've only had one date."

"But did you like her?"

A low laugh rumbled out of Mac and he shifted

uncomfortably. Like her? He hadn't been able to stop thinking about her ever since. Walking into the office and seeing her— "Yeah. I liked her. But if she's going to be my employee, that changes things."

"Well, about that…"

Chapter 9

V managed to avoid her father for the rest of her shift before heading out the door, but only because he and Mac were holed up in his office most of the time.

The customers and orders kept her busy, but all the while her brain rolled with the differences between working for her father in a business she *might* have inherited one day and working for someone else as an hourly employee.

If nothing else, the sale of Reels gave her even more incentive by pulling the safety net out from under her. Even though the net had felt more like a safety blanket and one she really appreciated because it allowed her to breathe when she thought of the future.

The moment she spotted Mac's broad shoulders reentering the restaurant, V said her goodbyes and flew out the back door.

Her father's condo wasn't that far of a walk, and despite being on her feet all day, she needed some fresh air to clear her head and formulate a plan. Step one was finding a studio she could train in during her nonworking hours. Step two was being able to afford studio time while not being a burden on her father.

At twenty-eight, she'd been on her own for some time. Paying her bills, making her own way. Scraping by on her dance pay by cutting every corner possible. But the injury had not only hurt her physically but financially. Like her father said, insurance only covered so much, and a dancer's salary—in New York, no less—was quickly eaten up by rent and essentials.

V made it to the end of the second block and was about to cross to the third when she realized she was no longer alone.

A vehicle crawled the otherwise empty street behind her and then wheeled into the parking spot she'd just passed. She heard a door open and turned to track the driver, but the lights blinded her. V quickly slid her hand into the outer pocket of her bag and grabbed her pepper spray.

"V, it's me."

Mac's broad shoulders and height blocked the blinding lights momentarily before they blasted her again. It took a moment for her eyes to adjust as he stopped in front of her.

His attention dropped to her hand and his eyebrows rose. "You gonna use that?"

"I'm still debating."

His lips quirked up at the corners, and she felt her heart tug at his handsomeness. Of all people, why him? "What do you want?"

"To talk. I told Vic I'd give you a ride home, but then you took off out of there before I could approach you."

The fresh air had only made the pain in her body more apparent after the long, busy day. "I'm not sure we have much to say."

"Really?" he said simply. "I disagree. Come on. Let me drive you."

V hesitated a long moment but then slid the pepper spray back into its appointed spot and retraced her steps down the sidewalk toward his SUV. Mac opened her door and held it for her. "Thanks."

"You're welcome."

"Should my boss be driving me home?" she asked as she climbed up into the seat. "Or does that just go with being a charity case?"

Mac didn't respond other than to shut the door, rounding the vehicle in long strides that ate up the distance and made her sigh with envy.

Seconds later, Mac climbed in beside her and fastened his seat belt then nodded toward hers. "Buckle up."

While she clicked the belt for the short drive, he got them moving.

"Look, V, I'm sorry for the way you found out about me buying your father's business. It shouldn't have happened that way."

She turned her face toward the window and a group of St. Patty's Day revelers outside slowly making their way back to wherever they'd hailed from. Mac drove well below the speed limit, and she understood why when a man stumbled out of the dark and into the street.

Mac hit the brakes and waited while the guy's date pulled him to his feet and back onto the sidewalk. "I should've asked if you'd been drinking tonight." She glanced at him. "Before I got in."

"I never drive drunk or buzzed. You're safe. And you're not a charity case."

She winced at the statement, wishing it was true. "I think being made part of your sale agreement nixes that idea."

"Look, Victoria, I know all of this has come as a shock, but I'm buying the business because it's a solid investment—and to help your dad. I hope you realize that."

"And entrepreneurs never take advantage of those in need of help," she murmured, her derision evident.

"Sometimes they do. But I made a fair and generous offer. Vic is a local and thought of very well here, not to mention a friend I've gotten to know in recent years. I'd only be hurting myself in the long run if the majority opinion was that I took advantage of him. I'd hurt myself and my investment if that were the case."

Mac's words seemed sincere.

"I just wish I'd known."

"That's understandable. But I think any decent parent tries to protect their child. You can't hold that against him. Not when he knew you were already dealing with your injury."

V pulled her cell phone from her pocket to check it and give herself something to do. She frowned at the face, realizing she'd missed a text from the dance studio on the island giving her available times, as well as... "Marsali called. Again."

"Are you going to call her back?"

"I'm not sure what to say. Especially now."

A light changed to red, and Mac slowed to a stop, turning toward her in his seat. "What would you have said before learning what you did tonight?"

She glanced at him and found herself drawn as always. "I'm... not sure. I mean, I had fun and enjoyed our date but..."

"But?"

"But if you're wanting to find someone and allowed Marsali to *match* you, I doubt you're interested in someone who has no plans to stick around. I'm not the person you want."

"And now I'm your boss."

"Yes." V tucked the phone away once more.

The light changed to green and Mac remained silent as he got them moving.

"What if you let me decide what I want?"

The words created a coil of heat in her belly, especially given the way he looked at her when he'd said them.

"I make a point of not dating employees. Mixing business with pleasure tends to make things complicated, and I've seen my share of businesses negatively impacted by it."

That it did. Ballet company romances were notoriously awkward. Working and playing together tended to make breakups disastrous. It affected performance, friendships. Everything.

"But as to your earlier statement… regardless of your intentions for the future, I'm interested. So if we were to do this—date—we'd have to set boundaries."

She blinked at his statement. "You just said you don't date employees. Are you *firing* me?"

Mac's husky chuckles filled the interior of the SUV. "No. But in light of the fact I would like to see you while you're in Carolina Cove, I made Vic another offer tonight. And he's accepted."

"Do I even want to know what that offer is?"

"I suppose it depends."

"On?"

"On whether or not you're using working for me as an excuse because you have no interest in me."

She knew better than to say too much too soon. "Go on."

His smile flashed in the darkened interior.

"The sale is going through as planned and will take a

couple of weeks to finalize things. But it will take the financial burden off of Vic and give him the cash flow he needs for his outstanding medical bills and finances."

"Okay."

"The second offer was a request for him to stay on and run the day-to-day as manager. He'll be a salaried employee with benefits, and since he knows the business inside and out, it just makes sense. Despite everything he's been through, he's kept the business afloat and doing well."

"If it's so lucrative, why not keep it?"

"You should ask him, but from what he's told me, he wants to take a step back. He can do that as manager since he won't carry the financial aspect of the business."

"I see," she said again. "What happens if he has another heart attack?"

"Vic's first order of business is to hire two assistant managers, one to focus on Reels and the other the charters."

"Sounds like you've thought of everything."

"I tried. But what that means, Miss Bartender, is if you screw up, Vic or one of the assistant managers will fire you. Not me."

A huff of a laugh left her at the warning, and she was all too aware of his gaze when he glanced across the vehicle, his eyes filled with unease as he waited for her response. "That's... good to know."

"I hope the extra layer of people between us takes the pressure off of us both, should we move forward and see each other privately while you're in town."

He made the turn into the condo's parking lot and pulled up beneath the canopied entrance.

"Whether you say yes or no, your job is secure. I trust Vic in that he wouldn't have hired you to tend bar if you couldn't keep up. He's a good guy, but he isn't stupid, and he had you working one of the busiest days of the year. So now you've heard my pitch… Go inside, think it over, call Marsali tomorrow, and tell her whatever it is you want to tell her about seeing me again in the future."

V gathered her bag but paused with her hand on the door latch, teeth pinching her inner lip as she gazed at him from across the vehicle. A moment of déjà vu slid over her as she exited, no closer to an answer than she'd been the first time they'd done this that night in the rain because, with his "pitch," he'd proven himself to be a gentleman. Again. "Thanks for the ride home—and for clarifying things. Good night, Mac."

"Victoria?"

"Yes?"

"We could have some fun while you're here. I hope you'll say yes."

Chapter 10

Mac entered his house after driving V back to her father's condo and tossed his keys into the bowl by the door for such purposes.

He stood there a moment, taking in the designer furnishings and decor that made the large house seem lonelier than the one-bedroom condo he'd lived in before.

He'd liked the idea of "bachelor row" as Marsali had named it when he'd moved between the two then-single Hayes brothers. The guys had introduced themselves, and Mac had made a point of inviting them to split the difference and hang out at his place when he'd seen them crossing back and forth to visit each other.

Hanging out had become the norm as months passed and the landscapers had completed transforming the outside, making his middle house a comfortable retreat Lincoln and Amelia had used as the backdrop for their wedding.

Now both brothers were happily married, and Mac found himself... bored. A man could only work so much without burning out, and he tried to maintain a good balance between work and play. He was successful, healthy… lonely. Which was why, when his best friend had gotten together with Marsali, Mac knew he had to take the next step and let Marsali work her magic and match him like she had so many other clients, his neighbors included.

V was a nice surprise. Looks-wise she appealed with her sultry dark hair. She was much too thin, but he attributed that to her profession. But what he knew of her personality—and her gorgeous eyes—drew him like no one had. Ever.

He'd had girlfriends, relationships, some lasting longer than others but mostly the kind that had fizzled out over time. It took a lot of hours and dedication to build the lifestyle he'd worked so hard to achieve.

He grabbed his laptop and settled himself into the oversized leather couch, sinking into the buttery-soft depths with a sigh. Despite his fatigue, he wanted to know more about V, and he hadn't really had a chance to research her until now.

Googling her was easy. Sorting through the mass of listings a little harder.

He clicked over to videos and began watching clips. Quite a few of the earlier videos left him straining to make her out among other dark-haired ballerinas, but the more recent ones he found left him watching in awe.

She flew across the stage, so light on her feet she seemed to literally fly. Graceful and fluid, her every movement somehow depicted the emotion of the music and the tale being told. She was *amazing*.

He watched more of her performances, shaking his head in wonder at how someone so tiny could be so powerful.

Her skills and presence outshined the other dancers,

and Mac remembered what Vic had said about her being prima ballerina.

V knew the type of dedication and work it took to create something from nothing. She understood it. It was yet another thing that appealed to him about her and made him want to know more.

What were her goals? Her plan for the next five years? Ten? Especially if she couldn't dance, as Vic had said. Something told him she'd thought it out. Planned it out. At least, she'd tried to.

That inner drive didn't just disappear, and Mac knew Victoria would channel that into other things. He couldn't wait to see what they were.

He clicked off the videos of her performing and moved on to other images and mentions. Mac frowned when he spotted a photo of her at a red-carpet event at the side of a blond-haired pretty boy.

Mac opened another tab and Googled the man's name, the screen quickly filling with Wall Street mentions and more pictures of the man, Parker Weatherington, as one of NYC's top thirty under thirty, as well as more images of Victoria and Parker together.

The two of them looked awfully cozy. Smiling for the camera and yet… where was Parker now? Knowing she struggled with a life-altering injury? Knowing she needed support as she healed and searched for whatever came next? Where was the man?

His phone buzzed on the cushion next to him and Mac picked it up to see Marsali's name. He tapped on the screen.

Hey. So, I still haven't heard from V. I'm so sorry. I'm not sure what's going on there with her. Do you want to wait and see… or move on to your next match?

He started typing but stopped. Waited. Why hadn't V called Marsali?

Mac?

He hit the erase and tried again before finally giving up and calling his sister. "Why are you working so late?" he asked when she answered.

"It isn't work when you love what you do," she stated, a smile in her voice.

"Oliver must love the late-night chats with your clients."

"Oliver isn't here, thank you very much. You know my rules."

Her rules. He admired his sister's rules. But mostly because her self-imposed relationship rules on no sleep-overs with the opposite sex and no commitment-less sex had kept him from bashing in heads or handing out black eyes over the years. "I'm just glad Oliver abides by them. Otherwise I'd have to have another talk with him."

Mac hadn't liked Oliver's involvement with Marsali. Not at first. When his buddy had made the decision to pursue a career in Hollywood with all its insanity, he'd given up his chance at a relationship with Marsali.

Ten years later, Marsali's on-air blunder stating Oliver was her perfect match had Oliver running to Marsali's rescue, and they'd fallen in love in the process. His buddy had chosen Marsali this time around, moving to Carolina Cove, where Oliver planned to work the local film industry as both actor and director/producer.

"Mac? Are you okay? You're unusually quiet."

"I just got back from driving V home."

"Oh. How did that, um, come about?"

His sister didn't like it when clients broke her dating rules, and he and V had broken several. All contact was to happen through Marsali at first, with no numbers or home addresses being exchanged.

He explained the situation with Vic as well as V's employment and the deal being made. Normally he kept quiet about such things until they were completed, but under the circumstances, he wouldn't mind Marsali's take. "So that's how I left it. She said good night and went inside."

"And you have no idea if she's receptive to another date? She didn't give you *any* indication?"

"No. I'd like to think she feels the same chemistry, but maybe I'm wrong and she doesn't."

"Do you want to pursue dating her if she has no intentions of staying?"

He stared at one of the images on the laptop screen, that of V in full costume, leaping into the air. "She's... different."

"I see. Well, I guess for now we both wait. Unless you have a better idea?"

Chapter 11

V entered the dance studio the following morning and welcomed the sight of the mirrored walls and wood floor off to her right. On the left was a single desk and, behind that, several doors and more glass-walled classrooms. "Hello?"

An older woman appeared, glasses perched on her narrow nose. V recognized the elderly woman as former dancer on sight. "Hi, I called about getting some studio time?"

"You're Victoria Valentine."

V blinked because of the way the woman said it, not naming V as the person who'd called for information, but because the woman recognized her on sight. "I am."

"I watched you perform last year in *Swan Lake*. You were magnificent."

V felt her resolve quake just a bit at the praise. "Thank you. I-I was told I might be able to get some studio time."

"Of course, my dear. We have a yoga class Monday, Wednesday, and Friday from eight until nine, and late-afternoon and evening dance classes for the children after school, but if the times on the wall aren't blocked, the room is available."

"And the rate?"

The woman's gaze narrowed once more, and she tilted her head to one side, looking at V over the top of her glasses.

"Perhaps we could make a deal. Studio time in exchange for your help with the students?"

"Oh, I'm not… I'm not a teacher."

"You dance. Quite well, I might add. You can teach."

"I have a job. Bartending. I'm not sure if I can—"

"We'll work around whatever hours you're not bartending. And in exchange, you'll get free access. How's that?"

Considering she'd wondered how she would pay for the time, anyway, V nodded. "Yes. Okay. I'll do it."

"Good." The woman waved a hand toward the room. "It's free now as you can see. I'll get you a key so you can come and go. It unlocks the main door only."

"Thank you. I don't know what to say— I'm sorry, I don't know your name."

"Gwendolyn Taylor," the woman said. "You haven't heard of me."

V smiled at the older woman, grateful for her kindness. "I have now."

"Well, what are you waiting for, Ms. Valentine? Get to work."

"V, I'm so happy to finally get to talk to you! How *are* you?" Marsali asked that afternoon.

V pressed the phone to her ear as she walked along the beach, able to ignore the chill in the air because of the glorious sunshine. She'd gone inside last night after Mac's statement but couldn't bring herself to make the call to Marsali until today. She needed time to think and sort things through and to do it without the cloudiness of pain and fear of whatever the future held.

But her time in the studio had only added to the questions swirling about in her mind because it had gone well. Really, really well. She'd seen quite an improvement since her last training session in New York. "I'm good."

"Yeah? I've heard there've been a few changes in your life recently. How are you doing with Mac buying your father's business?"

Wow. Nothing like getting straight to the point. "If that's what Vic wants, I'm good with it," she said, even though they were tough words to mean. "Look, Marsali, I'm sorry for not returning your call but I needed some time to think. Especially after my dad and Mac and everything."

"I understand. I'm sure it's a lot to take in."

"It is."

"If the buyer had been someone else, would it matter as much?"

"I… suppose not."

"So your hesitation is because you're interested in Mac and you'll have a business connection to him?"

"Yes. He's now my boss."

"Your boss's boss," Marsali corrected. "At least that's my understanding."

V laughed and paused on the sand, folding her legs to sit so she could stare out at the ocean. "I'm making too much of this—is that what you're saying?"

"No, you're not. You're concerned about crossing a boundary, and it's a legitimate reason for wariness. But it's also a place where you and Mac match on the moral scale, and as such, Mac made a point of keeping a layer of management between you. There's the fact that, according to your own words, bartending was just something to do while healing and training to return to New York, so we're not talking about you working at Reels forever."

"That's true." So why was she so hesitant? It wasn't like Mac was suddenly love-bombing her the way Parker had—up until he couldn't be bothered anymore because he couldn't get from her what he needed to uphold his narcissistic image.

"So… let's set that aspect aside for now and discuss the date itself. You had fun?"

"I did. Mac was a gentleman, as I'm sure you already knew."

"And your level of interest in Mac is what? No holding back. Days have passed without a word from you, and Mac could've easily moved on to his next match—yet he hasn't."

So maybe he wasn't at the undying love stage yet, but Mac had made his interest readily apparent in the way he'd looked at her. And when he'd driven her home just so he could clear the air? Reassure her that she would have a job for as long as she wanted one?

She didn't want to get hurt, but more importantly, she didn't want to hurt anyone else. There was more than enough of that in today's world.

"V? No more excuses. Are you going to give Mac a chance, or would you rather end things here so I can match him with someone else? The ball's in your court."

The image of Mac with another woman filled V's head, and just like that, jealousy reared its ugly head.

But how could she be jealous? She barely knew the man. Had shared limited conversations with him. But when she thought of him leaning down and brushing another woman's cheek with his lips… "No."

"No?"

"I… I don't, I mean…"

Silence. Marsali waited patiently and V struggled to gather her scrambled thoughts. This was why she'd postponed the call all this time, why she'd let Marsali's calls go to voicemail. "I don't want you to set him up with anyone else but—"

"But?"

"But I don't *know*! I don't know how long I'll be in town. I don't know if it'll work out between us or if a long-distance relationship would work at all. I don't *know* what I'm getting myself into, and I don't want anyone getting hurt."

Marsali's laughter filled V's ear, and she pulled the phone away for a moment to glare at it before placing it again. "Really?"

"I'm sorry for laughing. I *am*, truly. I *get* it," Marsali said, "but if you knew any one of those things, you'd be God and you're not, so, like the rest of us mere mortals, you're going to have to trust in what's meant for you working out."

The air left her lungs, and V scraped her fingers through the windblown tendrils blowing into her face. Marsali was right.

When had she become such a control freak? Or maybe she'd always been this way? After all, she hadn't gotten to where she had dancing without a lot of control and determination.

"V?"

She blinked back the sting of tears and blamed it on the wind and the pity in Gwendolyn Taylor's expression even as she'd complimented V on her performance.

But her time in the studio that morning? For the first time, she felt like she'd burst through the wall holding her back. Her body ached from the intensity of the workout, but it was a good ache. A familiar one.

She'd gone back to the condo and showered, changed for her first class tonight as a dance instructor, and yet found herself needing some time by the surf.

"Is something else on your mind? Some other reason you're hesitant?"

She opened her mouth and closed it again, needing to talk, to vent, to share. She'd had friends in the city, mostly dancers since those were the people she spent most of her time with on any given day, but since her injury, she'd discovered how lonely she actually was. It was like her so-called friends were afraid her injury would rub off on them, and one by one, they'd disappeared. And then there was Parker… "I dated someone in New York."

"The breakup you mentioned the first time we met? Are you talking? Getting back together?"

"What? No. No, I… I'm saying I dated someone. Someone who was important to me, but he couldn't handle my injury. Me having to use a cane after my surgeries, and him not liking what the doctors said about me and… my future. He wanted—desired—*that* part of me, not this one."

"He rejected you. I'm sorry. But, V, you do realize Mac has never *seen* that side of you and likes you just as you are. Right?"

Hearing Marsali state it so bluntly made V realize how trivial and ridiculous her words sounded. But dancing had been her identity for so long, she couldn't separate the two. Never wanted to. And yet, it was true. And the fact Mac liked her just fine as Vic's daughter and a bartender? The thought actually freed her from the weight of maintaining that image for one much less… intense.

Maybe during her stay in Carolina Cove, she could get to know that person, too. See herself through his eyes? Discover the woman at her core. "You're right."

She was who she was, injury and all. On her bad days, she limped. On her good days—of which she had far more now than bad—she danced. And she would continue dancing as long as she could.

She picked up a handful of sand and let it slide through her fingers. Cold, singular, tiny bits of shells and glass long lost to the wind and waves and sun. Pieces of a whole beautiful beach in minuscule form that reminded her of the metal bits now forming her leg—that would go on to do and be all that it could even in its mishmashed form.

"V? Did I lose you?"

She stretched her leg out and back before getting to her feet, dipping and turning, stretching, the movements as old and as familiar as the life it represented. "Set us up again."

"You're *sure*?"

She lowered into a slow plié, feeling the motion throughout her entire body. Today was a day of change. Mindset. Determination. Future.

Of trusting that, whatever happened, she would be okay. "I'm sure."

Because it was time to celebrate. And what better way to celebrate than agree to go out with a fantastic guy?

Chapter 12

The following evening, Mac headed home for a quick shower before picking V up for their second official date. He turned down the street toward his house when his phone rang. He frowned at the screen and pressed a button to connect the call through his Bluetooth. "Hey, Carter, what's up?"

"Mac, man, I need a favor. Can you pick up Piper? You're my last resort. I'm stuck in traffic while they clean up an accident, Eliza and Marsali are setting up a wedding across town, and my brother and Amelia are out of town visiting the kids," he said, referring to Lincoln's college-age twins.

Mac glanced at the clock on his dash and bit back a groan. "Now?"

"Yeah. Please, Mac, I'm out of options."

"I can but I doubt they're just going to hand your daughter over to a stranger."

"You're on the emergency pickup list. I added everyone the last time I got those papers."

"Okay. What's the address?" Mac asked.

Carter recited it and Mac nodded, well familiar with the building. It wasn't far from the restaurant where he'd planned to take V. "Any food allergies? I'm on my way to dinner."

"Ah, man, you're on a date?"

"Not yet but will be soon."

"I'm sorry. Seriously, man, if I had anyone else to call, I would."

"I get it. No problem."

"Text me the name of the restaurant and I'll be there to get Piper as fast as I can. Dinner's on me."

Carter ended the call, and Mac made a quick U-turn to head back toward the main road through Carolina Cove.

Mac slowed when he approached the shopping center and turned onto the lot. He spotted the numbers on the door and frowned. Dance class? He wondered how V would feel when he picked her up and found Piper in her dance clothes. Would V be bothered by it? Amused?

Inside the building, he waited for the parent in front of him to collect her child and pulled his phone from his pocket to text V and let her know he might be a few minutes late.

"Uncle Mac!"

Piper ran across the wooden dance floor into the lobby and wrapped her arms around his legs. "Hey, kiddo."

"You're my hero," she said, batting her baby blues. "Thank you for picking me up. Daddy said I'm to be extra good and to remind you to text him."

"It's my pleasure, sweetheart. How often do I get to take two beautiful girls on a date?"

"Daddy says I'm not allowed to date," Piper said. "*Ever.*"

"Well, maybe your daddy won't mind if I tag along."

Mac froze at the sound of V's voice and looked up to see her watching them from several feet away, amusement lighting her beautiful face. "Uh, hey."

She waved her phone. "I got your text."

He chuckled and tugged Piper along as he approached V. "Yeah, we have an addition to this evening. Is that okay?"

V winked at Piper and welcomed the girl's hug as Piper did her Piper thing and flitted about like the five-year-old she was.

"It's fine. Piper and I have had fun, haven't we?"

"Yup! Uncle Mac, watch."

Piper dumped her pink ballet bag and jacket and struck a pose, hands above her head, feet just so, and then twirled.

"Very good," V said.

"Wow," Mac drawled, eyeing V like candy when he had a massive sweet tooth. "So when did this happen?"

"Quite recently," V said, a flare to her icy-blue eyes and a twist to her full pink lips. "In exchange for studio time, I'm going to help out with a few classes—when I'm not bartending. The schedule is flexible," she said as though reassuring him.

He lifted his hands. "Hey, I'm not involved, remember? That goes through Vic."

V smiled at him while holding Piper's hands so the girl could twirl again.

"Hey, kiddo, are you hungry? Ready to go eat?" he asked.

"Can we have pizza?"

Realizing he'd opened the door to have their plans for the evening altered even more, he winced. "Uh, actually I thought maybe we'd go to—"

"Pizza sounds *wonderful*," V said, sliding him a tolerantly patient smile with more than a hint of coaxing. "I *love* pizza."

He wanted to protest yet another change to their evening, but considering he wasn't getting a shower or a change of clothes, not to mention they were taking along an imp, a casual pizza joint was probably best.

Mac caved entirely when both his dates blasted him with their beautiful blue eyes. "Okay, okay. Fine. Pizza it is. Let's go."

V grabbed her bag and fell into step at his side as they headed toward the door, and Mac wondered how she made a baggy, off-the-shoulder sweater and leggings look so sexy. "You look beautiful, by the way."

"Thank you. My wardrobe is kind of limited since I left New York with only a duffle."

"You definitely weren't intending to stay long, were you?"

"No," she said softly, "I'm not."

He took the statement in the present tense as a warning. "Got it. That means we'll just have to make the most of the time we have while you're here."

"That's what Marsali said, too."

Mac refused to let his thoughts about V get ahead of the present. V had made it abundantly clear she was interested in seeing him but that her time in Carolina Cove was temporary. He either had to deal with it or end things and allow his sister to match him again. He wasn't ready for that. So nice dinner dates, time spent together simply enjoying themselves. He was going to be happy with those things. Take it one day at a time with the companionship of a friend.

When he'd agreed to allowing Marsali to match him, it had been with the intention of finding someone long-term. Someone he might have a future with. But as Marsali had pointed out, he wasn't necessarily in a rush to get married, only to find companionship. And his interest currently walked next to him.

A round of giggles sounded from beside him when he passed a group of tweens.

Victoria's gaze followed the sound, and she smiled when she saw them. "You're in dangerous territory in here," she teased.

"So I see." They made it to the door, and he pushed it open for her and Piper to precede him. "Do you blush when you see me?" he asked when she brushed by him. "Because I really hope so."

V's throaty laughter and head tilt made him wish they were alone rather than in a building full of impressionable kids.

"Come on, hero. We're hungry."

Outside the building, Mac took Piper's tiny hand for crossing the parking lot. V slid her palm into his free one and squeezed. He walked between them, knowing this was what it would feel like to have a family one day. To be the man he hoped to be somewhere down the line.

Sometime soon?

V looked so tiny by his side, her head not even close to his shoulder, her body a fraction of his size given her ballerina weight. He was glad she carried pepper spray and made a mental note to have Carter check into martial arts classes for his tiny ballerina. One could never be too careful.

Twenty minutes later, the three of them sat around a table inside of his favorite pizzeria, and Mac watched Piper and V interact. They talked about dancing and mermaids and unicorns, and while his head whirled with the topics, V seemed to take it all in stride.

Her laughter and smiles drew the attention of the

other males in the restaurant, and Mac found his thoughts wandering.

To later, to the future. To that image he'd had so briefly while leaving the dance studio, even though he told himself he had to stick with the here and now because that's how V wanted things.

Carter appeared across the room and headed their way once he spotted Mac. Piper whined when she thought she had to leave without getting her pizza, and Mac reluctantly invited Carter to join them. It was one thing to have a cute kid along for their date but another to have Carter's knowing smirk sitting across the table. His friend and neighbor lived to get under Mac's skin.

"So," Carter said after Mac had introduced him to V, "a dancer, huh? How'd you meet Mac?"

"Marsali set us up," V said before Mac could stop her.

Carter's laughter filled the area and Mac felt his blood pressure rise. "Not a word. I mean it."

"Marsali set you… As in she *matched* you?"

"Knock it *off*," Mac growled.

Carter laughed until tears leaked out of his eyes.

"Daddy, why are you crying?" Piper asked.

As if sensing that Mac was about to plant his fist in Carter's face, his friend plucked his daughter up from the seat where she colored a placemat and pulled her over onto his lap. "Because Uncle Mac is funny."

"What's so funny about it?" V asked.

"Let's just say Mac has been anti-matchmaking for as long as the earth has been round."

V glanced up at Mac and then leaned into his side, staring up at him with an expression that left Mac struggling to suck in air.

"Mmm. So was I. But we know what we want and

what to expect from each other at this point. In that sense, I'd say we're a perfect match."

Perfectly *mismatched*, he thought silently.

Because if they were perfectly matched, she wouldn't be so dead set on leaving....

Chapter 13

By the end of the evening, Carter had taken Piper home after the five-year-old had her fill of cheese pizza, and he and V were able to finish their date alone. They talked about likes and interests, everything from television shows to travel experiences. She admitted to never having been on a Harley, and he promised to take her for a ride, liking the idea of her riding passenger to someplace special. He'd have to make that happen soon.

V excused herself to go to the ladies' room while he settled the bill, and he waited for her by the pinball and video machines. The space was unusually empty, and when he spied an old favorite, he slipped some coins into the slots.

"Boys and their toys," V murmured when she rejoined him. "I don't know about you. First Harleys and now games?"

He smiled at her and then groaned when it cost him the play. "You're a distraction," he told her. "Come here. Let's see what you can do."

"I've never played."

He blinked at her. "Ever?"

She shook her head, a smile lifting her lips at his incredulous tone.

"Ah, sweetheart," he said, tugging her over to stand in front of him and using it as the opportunity it was to wrap his arms around her. "That tells me you are in desperate need of a kiss," he whispered into her ear as he slid his hands down her arms to place her fingers on the buttons.

"A kiss?"

He chuckled, loving the scent of her hair and the way her slight body fit against him as he readied the game. "The name of the game," he said, lifting a finger toward the vertical part of the machine. "See?"

A throaty laugh left her.

"Well, and here I thought you meant the real thing."

He grinned and pulled back the lever that would send the ball rolling. "Oh, trust me, sweetheart, we'll get to that one, too."

MAC DID GET to that kiss. And then some, V mused the following morning when she rolled over in bed at her father's condo. A smile pulled her lips up when she thought of the fun she'd had on her second date with Mac. Turned out she was a natural at pinball, and their competitive sides came out—with winner's choice being the prize.

Mac ultimately won, but it wasn't until he'd walked her inside the building and they made it onto the empty elevator that he backed her into a corner and claimed his prize—that being a stream of kisses that left her breathless and clinging to him.

Still more kisses followed once the elevator arrived on her father's floor, and she was grateful Vic's neighbors weren't making any midnight runs to the grocery, otherwise they would've had an audience for their make-out session.

She inhaled and sighed, stretching her body against the cool sheets. She didn't have to work at the bar until later this evening, which gave her all day to get to the studio. She'd discussed the studio arrangement with her father yesterday, and since her focus had to be on training, they'd formulated a tentative schedule.

She was definitely receiving priority treatment and wondered how the other bartenders would feel about that when they realized.

The last thing she wanted was to cause trouble for Vic when he was in a new position as manager rather than owner. That had to be an adjustment for him as well.

A chime sounded and she rolled to grab her phone off of the charger.

Good morning, beautiful. I hope you slept well. Be careful in the studio and let me know how your day goes.

Well, wasn't that sweet?

She smiled at the phone, and even though she told herself not to invest too heavily in Mac or his interest in her, she flopped onto her back, phone in hand. **Good morning, hero. I demand a pinball rematch.**

The three dots appeared and she laughed softly.

Miss my kisses that much? I look forward to winning again.

Oh, a man and his ego. Not that she minded in this case. **Be warned, MacGregor Jones. I've got mad skills you can't even fathom.**

Her phone buzzed in her hand, surprising her so badly that she dropped it before she picked it up again to see Mac's handsome face. She'd sneakily taken the picture when he'd helped Piper with her pizza, the sight warming her heart. "Hello?"

"Tonight," Mac said simply.

"I work tonight. My boss is *so* demanding."

Mac's rich chuckle filled her ear and practically made her toes curl in pleasure. All from the sound? Oh, not good!

"I'll pick you up after your shift. One game. That's all I need."

"Oh-ho, you're *that* sure of yourself, are you?"

"Fine. If you win, what's your prize?"

She closed her eyes and rolled to her side, nuzzling her pillowcase. "I don't know yet."

"Well, let me know when you figure that out. In the meantime, enjoy your day, Victoria."

"No one calls me that."

A short silence followed her statement, and she worried her lower lip between her teeth, waiting him out.

"I do. Now go do whatever you have to do. The sooner it's done, the sooner I get to see you."

TWO HOURS LATER, V stared at herself in the mirror behind the barre as she breathed through the tears threatening to choke her.

She'd done it. Made it through the entire rotation and... *killed it* if she so herself. At least for a dancer just getting back into the game.

She shook off the lingering doubts plaguing her that she could indeed recover completely and turned to walk midway across the floor to begin again, the motions as familiar as her own body.

She ran through the dance sequence once more, had

long ago memorized until it was engrained in her muscle memory.

Once that was completed, she stretched a bit more, reminding herself that her body had been through a trauma and deserved time to heal and rest, before she faced the mirror once more.

She began again, this time running through the next bit, one that ended with a dizzying round of fouettés, her injured leg swinging out and then back in to spin again and again and again. Across the long expanse and back again, then once more toward the center.

She paused again, gasping for breath when her leg cramped. She paced the studio floor, stretching it out and massaging as much as she could until she resorted to going to the cooler she'd brought with her with baggies of ice.

"Bravo," Gwendolyn said as she entered the room.

V looked up and watched as the woman crossed the floor with a wide, malleable ice pack.

"I find these help."

V placed it on her thigh. "Thanks."

"They're kept in the small freezer by the exit in back. Help yourself any time you need them."

"How did you know?"

The older woman tilted her head toward the far end of the room, and for the first time, V noticed the camera positioned at the top.

"We had them installed after a parent claimed verbal abuse. The child went on to admit they'd lied, but I felt it prudent to have for the future."

Well, seeing as how ballet directors were often known to be tyrants at times, V hoped the kid's mom realized there was no protection in the real world.

"You're almost there, Ms. Valentine. Have no doubt."

V met the woman's gaze and blinked.

"I've studied your performances in the past, and again when you came here that first day. One would be hard-pressed to know you were ever injured."

Maybe. "Close isn't good enough."

"No, it's not, I suppose. But keep going. You'll get there."

A phone rang in the office and then buzzed at the woman's waist.

"I have to get this."

"Of course. Thank you. For everything."

Gwendolyn smiled and plucked the portable phone from her waist, answering the call with all the profession-alism and grace she displayed as she crossed the room toward the door.

After icing her leg, V did some stretches and floor work for flexibility before calling it a day. She gathered her things and walked home, entering the condo to shower before her shift.

She'd just finished getting ready and moved to the fridge to find a quick snack. As an employee, she could eat for free, and she saw a salmon salad in her future.

She ate some berries as she paced toward the condo's spacious sliding doors to get a look at the fabulous view. Her gaze fell on the computer bag shoved between the chair and the desk along the way, and she glanced at the door like a guilty child.

She tossed the last of the berries into her mouth and chewed while digging into the computer bag where her father had shoved the stack of bills the night of her arrival.

The stack was still there, seemingly untouched. Another indication of Vic's inability to pay until the deal with Mac finalized.

Neither her father nor Mac had shared the financial details of the sale with her, but both seemed satisfied. She had to think a marina-front restaurant would be worth quite a bit. Enough to allow her father to retire comfortably when his health demanded it?

She removed the stack and flipped through them, gasping at some of the amounts.

No wonder he hadn't wanted her to see them. Or to worry. But to have helped pay her many hospital expenses with these looming over him…

Something told her these weren't all the bills, either.

The lock turned and Vic walked in, catching her.

"Let me guess," he said, his voice gruff as he shut the door, "they jumped into your hands?"

Chapter 14

V stared at her father, the weight of the invoices, her day leaving her unapologetic. "I wanted to know how bad it was."

"Well, now you do."

"If you hadn't had to help me—"

"I didn't have to, sweetheart, I wanted to."

"But if you *hadn't* helped me," she said, "would you still be selling Reels?"

Vic inhaled and moved across the room to where she stood, enfolding her in his arms. She'd always loved his bear hugs and laid her head against his barrel chest.

"Yes, I would be. We're not talking chump change here, Tori. Your old man did all right. I've had my fun. I'm ready to take a step back and enjoy myself more. We only get so much time. The heart attack and your injury made me realize that."

She leaned her head back and stared up at him. "Will staying on as manager be too hard for you? Are you sure it's a good idea?"

"I'm sure. I agreed to do it as long as I'm able," he

said. "And I'm to start training assistant managers first thing so I can leave when I don't want to anymore."

Her father had always been a hands-on type of man. The type to work rather than play, which meant he'd spent far too many years inside that restaurant or running the charter business instead of enjoying the fruits of his labor. "Did you agree to stay on for my benefit as well?"

Vic squeezed her tight before setting her away from him.

"You are direct, aren't you?"

"Answer the question."

"Once I found out you two had dated, I knew Mac would get particular over the details. It's something I admire about him. I thought if I could get him to agree to keep me on, he might not end things right away."

"You're incorrigible."

"It worked, didn't it? Come on, I like the idea of clocking out at the end of the day and not having to worry about the ownership side of things. I didn't want him worrying over your employment status, so it was a win for us all."

"Dad—"

"Mac's a good man, Tori. I'd like to see you with someone good for a change."

"You never even met Parker."

"Didn't have to. The man left you in the hospital alone because of a party."

"It was business. He was expected."

"And you're still making excuses for his lousy treatment of you. Honey, you need a man who has his priorities straight. And you need to stop defending them when they don't."

She dropped her hold on him and stepped away. "Okay, fine. Parker was a jerk, but I wouldn't get your hopes up on me and Mac. We're… friends. I'll be going back to New York soon, and when I do… it'll be over."

Her father didn't comment on her statement but took the bills from her hands to put back into the computer bag.

"You are to stop worrying about these. I'll take care of them once the paperwork goes through and the money transfer is cleared at the bank. Now, you need a ride to work?"

"If you don't mind. I wanted to go early enough to get a salad."

"You need a steak. A big, juicy one, and a potato with all the fixin's."

"And you need fewer steaks and potatoes and more salads," she argued.

Vic huffed and crossed his arms over his chest. "Grab your stuff, skinny girl, and leave my diet to me."

Ten minutes later, V led the way into Reels with Vic behind her, laughing at some of the tourist antics taking place outside by the marina.

V heard someone call her name and turned, her laughter dying in her throat when she spotted— *"Mom? What are you doing here?"*

"Your father invited me. I hope that's okay?"

V couldn't believe her eyes. Or her ears. Her mom was here? *Invited by Vic?*

Why?

At forty-eight, her mother was beautiful. They shared the same dark hair and eyes, the same small build.

"Amy, you're looking good," Vic said.

"Thank you, Vic," Amy said, a frown pinching her features as she took in Vic's appearance. "I wish I could say the same. Are you okay? Have you been ill?"

"Ah, I'm fine."

V blinked, at a loss for words and yet… not. "Wait—you two have *talked*? Been in contact?"

"Your mother called me when you wouldn't return her calls," Vic said. "She was worried about you and how you left New York. We've chatted a few times since."

"I see. Thanks for the warning," V said.

"Now, Tori—"

"And he's not fine, Mom. He had a heart attack. In New York when he was there to see me. That's why he left… or didn't return to the hospital, I mean. He was in the hospital, too."

"For the love of— Tori, why would you go and—"

"*What?* Vic, why didn't you tell me?" Amy asked.

"No need. You were where you needed to be," Vic said.

"But you're okay now? Is he okay?" Amy asked V, her voice low, gaze filled with worry.

"Ask him." She'd always wondered why her mother and father had divorced. Her mom had said when Vic returned from the military, he wasn't the same man. That they were young and tried to make it work but couldn't.

Now years had passed, and her mother had remarried and been widowed, but it was pretty obvious her mother had unresolved feelings where her father was concerned. And Vic for Amy.

How had she missed those facts? Both asked about the other whenever V was around. Commented on each other's social media posts. Still, it had been a long time since V had seen the two of them together in the same room, and now that she had… Interesting.

V shook her head slightly at her rambling thoughts before shifting her attention to the man her mother had been sitting with. "Who's your friend?"

"Oh," Amy said. "V, this is Jonathan Frakkes. He's a reporter who wants to do an article on you."

The reporter had stood sometime during the earlier conversation and approached V with an outstretched hand.

"It's a pleasure, Ms. Valentine," he said, smiling as he shook V's hand. "I followed your rise through the company and have *always* been a fan. You're amazing, just amazing."

"Thank you," V said. "I'm not sure why you're here, though. I don't know anything about an article."

"That's because I just pitched it a few days ago. I contacted your roommates, who sent me to your mother, and she mentioned she was coming for a visit. I asked if I could tag along. How are you coping post injury?"

"I'm… fine. Training."

"That's wonderful. I mean, I pitched it as a human-interest story, thinking it would be a follow-up about whatever you do next but… I wouldn't mind a scoop, especially if you're planning a big comeback."

A big comeback? Press? Even more scrutiny?

What did you expect? To slide in unnoticed? "Mr. Frakkes—"

"Everyone in the ballet world has seen the video of the performance," he said, sliding her *that* look. "People were heartbroken by your injury and very concerned. A follow-up of any kind would be well received, but a comeback feature? 'Broken Ballerina Returns…' Oh, I can see it now."

"I think you're getting ahead of yourself, Mr. Frakkes," V said, anxiety riddling her attempts to breathe.

"I don't think so. Why train if you're not planning to return? Am I right?" he asked, sliding her a searching glance.

"Tori needs to eat," her father said gruffly. "The interview can wait. If she does it at all after the bad press she received."

"The memes," Jonathan said, nodding his head repeatedly. "Of course. Social media can be horrible, but I assure you, sir, my intentions are honorable."

"I'll think about it," V said, knowing the company was always receptive to *good* publicity.

"That's all I ask," Jonathan said. "My apologies if I've overstepped."

"You haven't," V told him. "I'm just surprised. Out of sight, out of mind and all of that."

"That's usually the case, but if you're about to come back after *that* fall, the article will help."

"Maybe."

The man's gaze shifted to her chest and he frowned. "Are you working here?"

"Actually, I am. Dancers do have bills, Mr. Frakkes."

"Jonathan, please. And of course. I'm just surprised. You mentioned training, so I automatically I thought, with all the time spent in the studio, you'd have little left over."

"I wanted to help my father."

"Yes. Did I hear something earlier about a heart attack?" the man asked, his gaze shifting to Vic.

"Jonathan, I have plans this evening, but how about we agree to meet tomorrow?" V said, desperate to get rid of the man before her father ripped his head off. "My mom has your contact information, right?"

"Yes, of course. My apologies. I get started with the questions and I can't stop. I look forward to chatting with you. You're missed in ballet. Truly missed."

If that was the case, where were her friends? Her director? The producer? After an initial call or two, they had all but disappeared. Because like it or not, in her line of work, when one dancer went down, there were many more vying to take the prima's place.

V pinned a smile on her face and patted the man's hand. "Thank you. I'll call you tomorrow morning to arrange a time to meet."

"You promise?"

Vic grumbled something under his breath, and V found herself silently agreeing. "Yes. Have a good evening, Jonathan. Enjoy your time at the beach."

V waited and watched as the man gathered his computer and travel bags from the table he'd occupied with her mother and lifted a hand as he left the restaurant. The moment the door closed behind him, Amy surged forward and wrapped V in a hug.

"I'm sorry. I know I got on your nerves and I truly didn't mean to. I want the best for you, always. I love you."

V squeezed her mother tight and nodded. "I know. I love you, too."

"You're moving well. Is the pain better now?" Amy asked, releasing V to study her face.

V nodded. "It is," she said, lifting her chin in defiance of the ache in her leg and the worried look in her mother's eyes. "Training is going well."

"Oh, V, are you sure you want to—"

"How about we go grab some food before she starts her shift," Vic said, ending what would undoubtedly be another round of *why can't you do something else with your life?*

Apparently sensing she treaded dangerous waters, Amy nodded.

"Of course. I'm hungry, too. Airport food is just awful. So, tell me," Amy said, looking up at Vic's tall frame. "A heart attack? How are you? Really?"

Chapter 15

Mac settled himself on the cushions in front of his outdoor fireplace and felt the weight of the stares from his friends. "Stop."

"No way," Carter said. "You teased us about Marsali setting us up; now we get to return the favor. Right, Linc?"

Mac glanced from one neighbor to the other and inhaled. "Where's Oliver and Marsali? The ladies? I thought they were joining us." So that he could be the seventh wheel yet again.

A rapid series of beeps and chimes and buzzes sounded as the men's phones went off.

"They are," Carter said, reading his. "Marsali texted everyone and asked if we'll meet them out front. Probably something to do with the wedding. God only knows what Eliza is going to do when it comes to planning a Hollywood star and a matchmaker's wedding."

They got up and made their way toward the front of the house when feminine shrieks echoed throughout the area.

Every so often, someone came across a snake or coyote

or other critter, or human, that caused alarm, but in this case, Mac spotted the females in his life shrieking and hugging while Oliver and two of his security goons stood watching in typical male bemusement.

Mac nodded at the men, glad Oliver was taking his sister's safety seriously. People weren't used to seeing a Hollywood star walking down the streets in Carolina Cove or Wilmington, and sometimes they got a little too excited —and close. With tourist season approaching and Marsali's own stardom growing as her matchmaking business soared along with her fame, the antics to get Oliver's and Marsali's attention had increased as they became the non-Hollywood "it" couple.

Marsali's best-selling dating book and connection to Oliver had made her an attention- grabbing celebrity in her own right, with another book being written, numerous viral interviews under her belt as a dating expert, and discussions of a potential talk show aimed at twenty-first-century dating and matchmaking.

Once the shrieks and laughter and hugs abated, Mac and the others stepped forward to get some answers. "What's all this about?"

"We're getting new neighbors," Lincoln's wife said.

It took a moment for the statement to sink in, and Mac looked at his best friend turned future brother-in-law. "Oliver?"

His buddy grinned and smiled as Marsali danced across the concrete driveway to hug Mac. "Hi, neighbor!"

"Seriously? You bought one of the houses at the end of the street?" The houses on that end were all rentals typically housing tourists or spring breaker types, but since the owners lived out of state, they didn't much care who rented so long as the check cleared.

"We did. Actually"—Marsali slid a glance over her

shoulder toward Oliver before turning back to face Mac —"we bought all three."

Mac looked at Oliver, who shrugged. "When it comes to security, it makes sense. And if you guys agree as the other homeowners, I have permission from the city to gate this end of the street since it dead-ends. The only access then is by water."

Carter chuckled and crossed his arms over his chest. "I think my property value just went up. Yeah, I'm good with it."

"Me, too," Lincoln said.

Everyone turned to look at Mac. "Yeah, sure." Whatever it took to keep his kid sister and friend safe.

"Let's celebrate," Amelia said. "I think we may have some champagne left over from our wedding."

"You should call V," Marsali said with a pointed look, sliding her hand through his arm. "Ask her to come celebrate with us."

He stared into Marsali's bright eyes and shook his head. "She's bartending."

Marsali's disappointment was visible.

"Well, how about instead we take the party to her?" Marsali said. "After all, we don't want to run out of champagne."

Mac looked up to find everyone in the group watching him, apparently already knowing the end result.

"Sucker," Carter said, grinning and earning an elbow in the ribs from Eliza.

"What about Piper?" Mac asked.

"Breanne came back with us today so she's home," Lincoln said, referring to his college-age daughter. "One of her friends is getting married, but Bre's hanging out with Piper tonight since we were going to be at your house."

"See?" Marsali asked, blinking up at him. "It's perfect. Let's go."

Since it was a beautiful spring night, they locked up the houses and regrouped out front to walk to the marina and Reels. The place wasn't crowded, and they chose to sit at the bar rather than a table.

As Mac took a seat, he noticed Vic over in the corner talking to a petite woman. The two looked pretty cozy.

"My mom," V said.

Mac turned to find V's ice-blue gaze as direct and compelling as always. And just as alluring. "The one you had to get away from?" he asked, having heard the story at the pizza place.

"That's the one."

"Are you okay?"

She planted her hands along the bar on either side of her and shrugged.

"Let's just say time will tell. Mom and I tend to be oil and water when it comes to my injury. She says… Well, we disagree."

"V, you have to meet everyone," Marsali said from beside Mac. "This is Oliver, my fiancé, you know Eliza— that's her husband, Carter, and Carter's brother, Lincoln, and his wife, Amelia. Everyone, this is V."

A round of greetings blasted her and V smiled. "Welcome. What is everyone drinking tonight?"

"Champagne," Mac said. "We're celebrating. Oliver and Marsali found a house," he said simply, not going into detail about how they'd purchased three. Would they combine them? Combine two and use the third as a guest house? Any number of scenarios was possible, and given the price of the homes here compared to California, he imagined Oliver had bought three for the price of one.

Something Mac admired about his longtime friend was

his business acumen, and while they'd kept the news quiet, Mac had an idea that the purchase had been in the works for a while.

"Congratulations. That's wonderful." V set to work getting flutes and finding a bottle of champagne, but as she poured her way down the bar and reached Amelia, Lincoln's wife held a hand over her glass.

"Water for me, please. Or ginger ale."

Silence settled amongst the group before everyone began speaking at once.

"Why didn't you tell us?" Marsali asked.

"*When?*" Eliza asked next.

"*How?*" Carter cried in a high-pitched voice like the ladies', giving them all an ornery grin and earning laughter from the group.

"Lots of prayer," Amelia said, and then to Carter, "and dedication," she added, blushing while sliding a seductive look at her husband.

"Do you know details? Due date?" Eliza asked.

"We get to throw a matchmaker *baby* shower!" Marsali said, looking dreamy eyed.

"Yes. But before that, a bridal *and* wedding shower for you guys," Eliza said.

Mac noticed the men looked more than a little underwhelmed by the shower glee shared by the women and struggled to keep his amusement to himself, watching V as she went on to fill Amelia's glass with ginger ale and then finish off the last of the champagne flutes. "Get one for yourself," Mac urged her.

"We came here just so we could include you," Marsali added with a smile.

Mac frowned at V's response because, yeah, her expression said it all. She was taken aback by the act. The thoughtfulness?

Or was it because she was all for keeping things casual, and here they were bombarding her in a very public way because of her connection to him?

No pressure, right?

Maybe they shouldn't have brought the party here, but he'd liked the idea of seeing her. Especially if it meant he could tug her into someplace private and kiss her like he had last night.

So much for setting and keeping boundaries.

V composed herself and smiled, pouring a flute for herself and holding up her glass while Carter congratulated his brother on impending fatherhood. Once that sip had been taken, Mac lifted his glass to congratulate his sister and best friend on their impending homeownership, welcoming them to the neighborhood.

At that point, Vic approached to welcome and greet them, and Mac noted the way the man's gaze kept returning to the woman who remained at the table across the room.

As Vic continued on through the restaurant, checking in with the other patrons, Mac turned toward V. "I didn't hear from you after your studio time today. How did it go earlier?"

"Yeah, sorry. I was going to, but things got a bit crazy with my mother showing up with a reporter in tow."

He noticed she'd avoided the reference to her dancing but allowed it due to his interest in the rest of her statement. "Reporter?"

V rolled her eyes and gripped the towel in her hands until her knuckles turned white.

"Yeah. He said he wants to do a follow-up story on me. Some kind of human-interest thing."

"Is that what you want? If not, you can always say no," he told her.

"I could. But… maybe it would be a good thing to agree. I mean, it could help my visibility, be good press, that sort of thing. Maybe the article and the interest it would bring to the company could help me get back on stage long enough to prove myself again."

He waited, silent.

Seconds later, she sighed.

"Is this weird for you? Listening to me talk about leaving?"

He stared across the bar at her and wondered how honest he should be. "I don't like it, but I've always been a believer that if something is meant for you, it'll happen. I guess I have to apply it in this case as well. It's been a long time since I've found a woman fascinating enough to ask for second date. You intrigue me, Victoria."

She blinked at his statement and her lips parted.

"You just liked having two ballerinas on your arm last night."

He chuckled and nodded. "Can't argue that. Especially one in particular." He leaned forward on the stool and contemplated the woman across from him. "If your ballet company won't give you a chance to prove yourself based on your history with them alone, they're not the place for you."

"That's… I don't know about that. They want the best, so who can fault them after my last professional performance, you know?"

"We'll agree to disagree," he said, holding her ice-blue gaze. Sensing she wanted a change in subject, he winked at her. "So when do I get to meet your mother?"

Chapter 16

V was well aware of the moment her mother fell in love with Mac. After stating his question and pestering her for the next ten minutes until she complied, V finally motioned for her mother to join the group at the bar.

Amy slid onto the stool on the other side of Mac, and V poured her a glass of champagne as well, introducing her mother to the entire group, saving Mac for last.

"You're as beautiful as your daughter," Mac said to Amy. "It's nice to meet you."

"Hands to yourself, Romeo," Vic said as he joined them. "You've already got one of my women."

Her mother's eyes widened when she understood the context of the statement. She lifted her glass and toasted V and then blasted Mac with typical motherly questions.

What did he do? Oh, he owned compan*ies*. Where did he live? Oh, a house on the waterway. With every answer Mac provided, her mother slid V a look that begged her not to let Mac slip away.

Someone turned up the music, a few of the patrons began to dance, and V doled out drinks while enjoying the show. That is, until her father asked her mother to dance and the two looked like teenagers.

"Gonna catch flies," Mac said.

She shut her gaping mouth, blown away by the tender way Vic stared down at Amy, and knocked back the last of her champagne like the shot she'd rather have. "I'm just… What's happening?"

Marsali giggled. "Romance. *Romance* is happening. I love romance," she said dreamily.

"You are such a lightweight," Eliza said, rolling her eyes. "One drink and she's toast."

Oliver grinned and nodded as he got to his feet.

"Come on, Miss Romance, let's go show them how it's done."

"We can practice for the wedding!"

V watched as Oliver led his bubbly fiancée to the dance floor and drew her close. Before long, the other men had taken their wives out onto the floor, and Mac sat alone at the bar.

"The only dancer in the place and she isn't dancing," he said softly.

Her heart warmed at the look in his gaze and she shrugged. "I've danced today so I'm good."

She winced, wishing she'd kept the comment to herself. Mac had asked how things had gone earlier, and she'd managed to avoid answering. As to his statement about the company where she'd danced… "I'm fine. Actually, better than fine. Today was a good day." She glanced around, uncomfortable with the expression on Mac's face. "I, um, have to take these empties out. Be back in a bit."

She lifted the bin of empties and headed toward the rear door.

Mac's hands slid over hers at the end of the long bar

and he took the bin from her. "This is about as heavy as you are. Where do you put them?"

"I can carry—"

"Where do you put them?"

She released the bin and turned, leading the way out the back to where the empties stayed until pickup.

Mac shortened his long strides to match hers, and once his hands were free, he snagged her arm and tugged her to him.

"Hi," he said simply.

He bent his knees and lowered his head so that he could kiss her, and she held on to him when one kiss led to several more before he lifted his head, his large palm cradling her face.

"What are you thinking?"

She inhaled, staring into his dark green eyes and feeling her defenses crumble. "Your friends are nice."

"I kiss you and you're thinking about my friends?"

"You're nice," she said, ignoring the teasing tone. "I don't want to hurt you, Mac, and if you're looking for something serious—"

He pressed another kiss to her lips and stopped her words, lingering until she almost forgot them.

"Let me worry about me. Okay?"

She nodded and stood on tiptoe to kiss him again, giggling softly when he grabbed her behind and lifted her up to sit atop the railing along the marina. "Are you throwing me back?"

His husky chuckles warmed her insides, and she clutched his shoulders even though she felt secure in his embrace.

"You're awfully small. I just might."

The extra height brought her gaze level with his, and she slid her hands from his shoulders to around his neck.

"You know, my boss better not catch me out here with you or I could get fired."

"I have an in with him," Mac said, nibbling her lips. "You're safe."

"Mm, but am I?"

"Safe from him… not from me."

She shrieked softly when he pretended to drop her and then grab her again, swinging her up and then setting her safely on her feet in front of him.

"Come on. Better not be out here too long or Vic will have my head."

"You know, it's probably not good when the owner is scared of the manager."

Mac chuckled. "Only where you're concerned, sweetheart."

Mac pulled her close and kissed her one last time, lingering in the shadows of the building.

"I can hold my own, you know," she breathed when he finally let her up for air.

"We'll see. Especially after our rematch later."

"Hmm. Would you be as interested in a rematch if I was just a friend?"

She watched as his gaze lowered to her lips, and she couldn't stop the flick of her tongue to wet them, earning a husky groan from him, even though she ducked beneath his arm and scooted away.

"Victoria?"

"Yes," she said, sliding him a glance over her shoulder.

"Where are you going?"

"My shift was over twenty minutes ago. I'm going to play pinball."

THE FOLLOWING MORNING, V inhaled and picked up her pace as she jogged along the sidewalk, her mind still reeling from the fact that she'd introduced Mac... to her mother.

On top of that, when she'd returned to the condo after playing—and losing—pinball with Mac, she'd discovered her mother and Vic sitting side by side on the couch together watching television like in some surreal fifties sitcom.

Her mother had been beside herself about V's newfound friends, but when the discussion turned to her relationship with Mac, V had quickly excused herself to go shower before bed.

V thought her mother was going to lose her mind about Mac. And why not? After all, what better way to get her daughter's mind off of dancing and the doctors' gloomy prognoses than a gorgeous man?

V pushed harder, knowing her stamina had suffered over the last six months and she needed to build it up.

She'd called Jonathan Frakkes this morning as promised, but the call thankfully went to voicemail. On her way out the door, her watch buzzed, announcing Jonathan's return call, but this time she let it go to voice-mail, not wanting the man's questions in her head as she tackled her workout.

Sixty minutes later, she braced her hands on her hips as she approached the beach access that ramped up over the dunes, needing some salt air and surf to counter the rampant thoughts clouding her brain.

Her workouts were going well. She was having less pain than ever. Her studio training was getting better and better.

But when was it time? When would she be ready? *Know* she was ready?

Would she always wonder? Wonder if she was as good as before? If she was ready to go back and endure the endless training and grueling work required? After training all of these years, sacrificing nearly everything in order to put dance first, why was she doubting… everything?

Even she knew she could and would go as far as her mindset allowed her to go. That was the key.

The bite of the blustery wind didn't diminish the fact Carolina Cove was way warmer than New York, even though she needed the thin down vest she wore over her running gear when she topped the dunes and the full blast hit her.

She made her way to the packed sand and took a look around. It was early yet. And other than a blob in the far distance that looked to be several people, she had the beach to herself.

She took position and lifted her hands, slowly weaving her way along the sand, swaying, dipping, fast, quick steps that made up the routine she knew by heart. The warmup began slow and steady, then grew increasingly harder, faster, until she rose to her toes and—

With a gasp she went down to her knees, the sharp jab of pain coming out of nowhere and nauseating her with the intensity. She focused on her breathing until it passed and rolled to her hip and stretched out her injured leg, massaging the cramp.

As quickly as it had appeared, it was gone, but aftereffects lingered. If that happened when she was on stage…

It wouldn't.

It couldn't.

The only reason she'd cramped up at this point was because she'd let her thoughts venture into the darkness of doubt and trepidation instead of standing strong in her belief that she could do this. She could do anything. She was freaking Wonder Woman.

"V? That you?" a voice called, his tone sharpening. "V, are you okay?"

V lifted her head to find Mac and Oliver Beck, as well as one of the bodyguards who had accompanied the group to the bar last night, running toward her. All three of them staring at her with varying expressions of concern.

Apparently the blob in the distance she hadn't been able to make out had been the three of them jogging along the beach. Seriously, could her luck get any worse? "Yeah. I'm fine."

"You sure about that?" Mac asked, hurrying to where she sat on the sand.

He folded his long legs and knelt beside her.

"May I?"

Only then did she realize her fingers literally clenched into her leg. The pain was gone but her anger remained. "I'm good."

"V? Victoria," he said softly. "Let go. Let me help." He gently shoved her hands away to dig his own fingers into the muscle of her thigh.

"It's gone now."

"This will help," he said. "I played basketball all through school and used to get the worst leg cramps."

She lowered her head, chin to chest and eyes screwed tight, as he massaged her leg. She stared out at the surf, and it took everything in her not to release the tears welling up, inordinately grateful for the wind that dried any evidence of those that did.

Seconds passed that felt like hours.

"We'll go get a vehicle. Come back to get you," Oliver said.

"No, it's fine. I'm fine," she said, shaking her head. She

didn't want a fuss. She *hated* people making a fuss. Especially over this.

"Text me when you head our way," Mac said, countering her words.

She glared at them, but since it meant the men were no longer standing there staring at her, she decided to let it go.

Mac continued to work on her leg for another minute or so until she pushed his hands away. "Thanks. I'm good."

"You sure?"

She was more upset that the cramp had appeared than anything. Dancers got cramps all the time, but she knew it would be looked at differently with her. It was a flaw, not simply the norm.

"V? Come on, sweetheart, what's going on in that beautiful head of yours?"

A huff left her and she felt the emotions welling up in her again. "I psyched myself out," she said simply.

"Pardon?"

"I was thinking about dancing and New York and my injury and how important it is that I prove *every*one wrong, and that happened. Because for a split second I doubted myself and— "

"You lost focus."

She nodded and lifted her lashes, forced herself to meet his gaze. "I can't just go back. I have to return better and stronger, and if a single thought can do *that*... If it happens on stage... Again?"

Her voice broke and she cleared her throat, shaking her head. "Ballet is laughed at as a sport, but the level of training and endurance... Did you know the NFL is now using ballet as part of their training regime? To build endurance and stamina."

"I didn't."

"I can't let a single thought psyche me out. Not if I'm going to do this. If I'm going to *be* Victoria Valentine."

"Sweetheart, you are Victoria Valentine. Nothing can take that away from you."

"Falling made me look weak. Inept."

"Falling made you real," he countered. "Human. Why else would the reporter be here wanting to follow up? It's because people identify with *that* person, not the picture-perfect dancer but the woman she is beneath the costume and lights."

She wanted to ask the question on her mind. The *what am I going to do if* question that he wouldn't be able to answer because only she could. But the fear? The gut-curling panic she felt that she *wouldn't* be able to prove the doctors wrong?

It was real and tangible in the worst possible ways.

Mac shifted until his back was to the wind, and he blocked her from the worst of it. He stayed there, kneeling on the sand in front of her, holding her gaze with an expression that tugged at her heart.

"If it's meant for you, it'll happen," he said simply. "Focus on that. Nothing else."

"It's that easy for you? What about all the work? The *years* of training every single day—" Her voice broke and she swallowed hard. "What if you woke up tomorrow and every business and investment you own was just… gone. Poof. Would you really sit there and say it wasn't meant for you or would you be as mad as I am right now?"

Several seconds of silence passed.

"No, you're right. I would be. If that happened, I'm not sure what I'd do except… start again. That's all we can do. All any of us can do."

Start again. She was trying. Trying hard.

But what happened if trying wasn't enough?

Chapter 17

Mac pondered V's words, unable to get them or her heart-breaking expression out of his head. Playing ball in school wasn't the same as competing on a professional level, but he knew how dangerous one's thoughts could be if left unchecked.

His phone had beeped, alerting him to the fact Oliver and Denz were on their way with a vehicle to pick them up and take V home.

He'd stood, helped her up, and bent to scoop her up when she'd scrambled out of the way, determined to make her own way as she mumbled about fuss. Halfway to the beach access point that crossed up and over the dunes, she paused and leaned against his side, her arm sliding around his waist as she tried to maneuver the soft, shifting sand. On two healthy, uninjured legs, it was said to be a workout. For someone in pain, it was like quicksand.

He bent over her slight frame and kissed her head. "Hate me later," he said as he scooped her up.

She tensed but didn't argue, a sure sign of the mindset she struggled with at the moment.

Mac carried her across the sand to the wooden planks and up the steps before lowering her to her feet. He stood several steps below, putting them eye to eye much like they'd been last night near the marina.

The wind blew her long hair into her face despite the headband she wore, and he lifted his hands, brushing it back and cradling her small face in his palms. He brushed his thumb over her lower lip to dislodge yet another tendril of hair and lowered his head slowly. To let her pull away, push him away. Decide the next few seconds the way she so desperately wanted to decide her future.

When his lips met hers, the wind and the world disappeared in a rush of heat. She tasted like minty toothpaste and salty tears, of warmth and sunshine and something indefinably her.

Mac felt her arms slide along his neck, and he pulled her closer, protecting her from the wind while kissing her like a drowning man desperate for air and she was the source. She was torn between her present and what she wanted it to be, and so was he.

The crunch of gravel alerted him to someone pulling into the parking lot, and he lessened the intensity, ending the kiss but just as quickly pressing one more to her full lips as he glanced up to see Oliver's black SUV pull in, Denz behind the wheel. "They're here. Come on."

They crossed the bridge and descended the steps, silent now that the rush of words and kisses was over.

Mac opened the door and climbed in behind her, thanking the men for coming to get them.

"Yes. Thank you," V said, her voice soft, gaze averted as she stared out her window.

Mac gave Denz directions to her father's condo, and in a matter of minutes, they pulled beneath the entryway.

"Don't wait on me," he told them. "I'll find my way home."

He exited the vehicle and watched as V hesitated before scooting across the seat once more.

"Thank you," she said again.

"V," Oliver murmured. "I'm new to the Wilmington film community, but I'm always on the lookout for talent. If you're interested, let me know. I'll see what I can do."

"That's… very generous of you. Thank you," she said.

V looked at Mac and he felt her gaze like a punch to the gut. She got out and headed toward the door, and he fell into step at her side. "I didn't put him up to that if that's what you're thinking."

"I wasn't… but I'm glad you didn't."

She paused at the top of the steps.

"If you need me to, I'll carry—"

"No," she stated firmly. "I just needed… My mom's going to be inside. Can we not mention… what happened? I don't want to get into it with her."

Mac had a feeling her mother would be able to sense V's upset either way. "Of course."

They made their way through the lobby to the elevator. Once inside, she leaned against the wall and he found himself under intense scrutiny. "What?"

"Thank you. For helping me."

He braced his hands on either side of her and liked the way her eyes widened just a tad. Not out of fear but desire. "I can think of another way you can thank me."

Her long lashes lowered as well as her gaze, and he took advantage of the moment while he could, sealing their lips in a repeat of the kiss, only deeper, sweeter. Until the world disappeared altogether.

"Ahem."

Mac lifted his head at the unknown voice and turned to find the elevator doors open and Vic standing there looking very much like a protective father while V's mother looked wide-eyed and ready to jump for joy. "Uh, hey. Didn't know we'd arrived," he said, taking a step back.

"I think that much was obvious," Vic grumbled.

"I have to say you two do make a pretty couple," Amy said.

"Mom, stop. We're just… friends," V said, glancing at Mac before quickly looking away.

The elevator doors began to close, and Vic and Mac both shoved their hands out to stop them. He waited for V to exit and followed before the older couple got on the elevator.

"Where are you going?" V asked her parents.

Amy looked up at Vic, a smile on her pretty face.

"Your father has asked me out to lunch."

"Like… a date?"

Amy grinned.

Mac was aware of V's expression shifting to one of shocked surprise before her father chuckled and loosed the elevator door.

"Mac, be good to my girl."

"Always," Mac said. "Enjoy your lunch."

They stood there while the elevator doors closed with a soft snick of sound. "You couldn't look more shocked."

"I don't think I could *feel* more shocked. Twenty-four years later and they're… dating? Seriously?"

He chuckled and turned to follow her down the hallway. "When it's right, it's right."

"You said that because you don't want to repeat your mantra about it being meant to be so soon."

"It's more than a mantra." He bent and casually swept her up in his arms.

"What are you doing?"

"Enjoying myself," he said.

"I could walk faster than this," she said, sliding her arm around his neck.

He bent his head, lifting her at the same time, and nuzzled. "But I wouldn't be able to do this," he said, kissing her just beneath her ear and earning a shiver that ran through her body.

She angled her head until her mouth was close to his.

"Mac… what are we doing?"

"Enjoying a leisurely walk," he said, knowing she would consider any other statement to be a form of pressure. Something *she* didn't need at the moment as she sorted out her post-injury life… and thoughts.

"You know what I mean."

"Well, considering we've had one first date, and our second date was crashed by a five-year-old, I think it's fair to say we're taking steps to get to know one another, and a third date is in store."

As soon as the words left his mouth, the age-old adage appeared in his head about the same time her eyes widened, an indication she'd had the same thought. "Just a date, Victoria. No pressure."

They'd made it to the door but he didn't set her down. "I know you're dealing with a lot. And have even more to figure out. Am I right?"

A short nod was his answer.

He kissed her, keeping this kiss light and easy, just enough to tantalize and torture them both before he lowered her feet to the floor. "You're not working at Reels tomorrow. I checked the schedule. Spend the day with me?"

"I have to train."

"After your workout," he said, never wanting her to think she had to choose between the two.

"Maybe. Can I let you know?"

Chapter 18

V showered and iced her leg before responding to Jonathan Frakkes's voicemail. They agreed to an afternoon coffee meeting at London's Lattes before she had to go to the studio for the children's classes this evening.

V Ubered there and arrived a few minutes early. She smiled at the friendly woman behind the counter and ordered a mocha before making her way to a table in the far corner, hoping it would give a modicum of privacy.

Jonathan arrived within a few minutes after V had received her order and quickly joined her.

"Thank you for meeting me. I wasn't sure you were going to after we played phone tag."

"To be honest with you, I wasn't sure I was going to, either," she said, watching as he settled himself in with coffee and notepad and a recorder. "Leave that off, please. This is strictly a meeting to see if I *want* to do an interview."

Jonathan hesitated momentarily but then made sure she saw that the recorder wasn't running before he put it back in the computer bag.

"Okay, so… how are you? Really."

She laughed softly and blinked at the man. "Straight to the point."

"I find it's best for everyone. Takes the guesswork out of things."

"I'm good," she said, meeting his gaze and holding it. "Healing. Getting better day by day. How long have you followed ballet?"

Jonathan smiled and tapped his pen against the notebook.

"I took lessons during my formative years. Until the bullying got to be too much and I quit. I never stopped following it, though. I pursued journalism as an alternative creative outlet, and I found I could combine the two. Why hesitate over a simple interview?" he asked next.

"Wouldn't you hesitate if your last public appearance had gone viral?"

Jonathan acknowledged that with a wry dip of his head.

"I suppose so. But I assure you I don't intend to paint you in any negative light. You were the star of your company. People are curious about you. Concerned. And I've always liked an underdog."

Given the term—the tone—she struggled to keep her poker face. "What do you mean?"

Jonathan inhaled and sat back in his chair. "For all the HIPAA requirements, news gets out. Orderlies, food delivery, janitorial staff… People hear things. And they talk."

Her fingers tightened over her cup, and she cringed when she saw Marsali and Oliver entering the coffee shop. "Everyone talks. That doesn't mean what they say is true."

"I hope it isn't. Because what *they* say is that doctors said you'll never dance professionally again."

V forced a smile when Marsali spotted them. The

woman's gaze narrowed and apparently noted that Jonathan wasn't Mac, and V prayed when Marsali approached the table that Marsali wouldn't comment on how Oliver and friends had come to her rescue just that morning.

"Hey," Marsali said, bending to hug V. "I just wanted to come over and say hi."

Jonathan stood and V made the introductions.

"Wait a minute, you're the matchmaker"—Jonathan's attention immediately shifted to Oliver's incognito-ed sunglass-and-beanie-wearing presence across the room, as well as the bodyguards in attendance—"engaged to Oliver Beck."

He glanced at V and she shrugged. "I'm not the only story in town, you know. Maybe you'd have better luck with them."

"You're a reporter?" Marsali asked.

"I am," he said, giving his credentials. "Have you known each other long?" Jonathan asked. "Are you a fan of Ms. Valentine's?"

"We met at Reels," V said before Marsali could speak and potentially out her as a client in her database. "When I was bartending. Marsali and her wedding planner were there, and we wound up girl chatting."

Jonathan's attention focused on Marsali and V shook her head in warning.

"I see. Any fun, fabulous details you'd care to share about the wedding?" he asked.

"Only that it'll be fun and fabulous," Marsali countered without pausing. "It was nice to meet you, Mr. Frakkes. V, call me later?"

"Sure."

"Wait… I'd love to meet your fiancé," Jonathan said, his hand shooting out to stay Marsali's exit.

Denz and Oliver both closed ranks in a split second, and Jonathan quickly released his hold, backing up a step until his leg hit his chair and it grated against the floor. "No offense. Sorry. Sorry. Just wanted to meet you," he said to Oliver, hands held up. "My apologies," he said, introducing himself all over again.

Oliver draped an arm over his fiancée's shoulders and stared at Jonathan. "You're here for a story on V?"

"Yes. That is, if she agrees," Jonathan said. "We're… ironing out specifics."

"We'll leave you to it then," Oliver said.

"I'd love to also interview the two of you while I'm here. Get an idea of how the hottest couple is settling into Carolina Cove?"

"We'll see how V's article goes first," Oliver said. "Marsali, we have to go."

"Sorry," Marsali said. "Catch up with you later," she said to V.

Jonathan seated himself once more and made a face, having apparently realized Oliver wasn't interested in chatting any time soon and he had to settle for the non-Hollywood dancer.

"Well, I will say this, you work fast, Ms. Valentine."

"Oh? How so?"

"You've been here what? A few weeks? Yet you've made friends with Oliver Beck and his influencer girlfriend."

"Jonathan, what do you want from me? Besides answers I may or may not be willing to give?"

"I don't know. Maybe some time in the studio while you train? Photographs as you practice? I've watched so many of your performances pre-injury, I'd love to see how you're doing now."

"You can't simply take my word for it?"

There. Right there, she knew what she was up against. That look, that flicker of expression that crossed his face before he hid it told her exactly what she wanted to know. Needed to know. Convince him, and he would convince everyone else. And in doing so, she would get her toe shoes back in the door of the company she hadn't heard from in months. It really would be the performance of a lifetime. Should she take it on. "I'll think about it."

"Think about it? I was hoping for an answer today, Ms. Valentine."

"I don't doubt you were but… I'm not convinced the article will be a positive one."

"You have my wor—" He broke off, smiling slightly. "Yeah, I heard that, too. Okay. So, how do we come to terms?"

Chapter 19

"Uncle Mac? What are you doing here? Are you picking me up again?" Piper asked, a perplexed expression scrunching up her adorable face when she spotted him walking into the studio's waiting area.

Mac ruffled her little red head once she got close enough and winked. "No. I'm here for your teacher." *Hot for teacher* was more like it. But that wasn't something to say to a five-year-old.

"Mrs. Taylor?" Piper asked, going wide-eyed.

Mac coughed and shook his head. "No, sweetheart. I meant V."

"Oh. She's teaching the big kids now."

"I see. What room are the big kids in?" he asked, following her pointing finger to the room farther down the lobby.

As though she sensed his gaze, V lifted her head, and their eyes met through the classroom's glass.

She continued saying whatever she said to her students, moving them through a series of complicated steps he couldn't begin to follow.

Mac also noted a man in the room taking photos. V's class, made up of five girls and one boy, looked to be taking things pretty seriously. Maybe due to the photographer. Maybe due to their teacher gently correcting them when needed.

Eliza appeared and he nodded to the woman who'd quickly stolen his neighbor's heart and charmed his precocious daughter. "There's Eliza," he said to Piper.

"I call her Mommy now."

He blinked at the announcement and squatted down to be at eye level with Piper. "Wow. That's a big step. I bet she likes that."

"She does," Eliza said, smiling as she joined them.

"It made her cry at first, but she said they were happy tears," Piper added.

Mac smiled and straightened. "I'm sure they were, sweetheart."

"What's going on over here?" Eliza asked.

"Mommy, here. It's about our show," Piper said, holding out a paper for Eliza to take. "V's going to dance in it."

Mac couldn't see the details on the sheet all the kids carried, but an excited buzz filled the area where everyone amassed to find their parental people.

"Oh, very cool. Hey, Piper, give me a minute alone with Uncle Mac, okay? Stay close, though."

"Okay. I'll say goodbye to Madison."

The little girl took off, and Eliza regarded him with a tilt of her head and a flash of too knowing gaze.

"She must be feeling better if she's dancing in the program," Eliza said.

"Yeah. Great news."

Eliza crossed her arms over her front and cocked her

head. "Uh-huh. Don't you have a job or a corporation or two to run?"

He waved the phone in his hand. "Ah, see? They have these little handheld computers now that pretty much allow me to work from anywhere."

"Anywhere being a dance studio?"

He smiled slightly and shrugged. "When needed. Shouldn't you be going home to a certain contractor right about now?"

"Oh, trust me. He'd want the details of my seeing you here. Are you thinking of taking a class?" she asked with an innocent blink.

He took the teasing in stride and decided to make use of the feminine company until V's session ended. "What can I say? I like her."

"Um, I think we *all* see that. So are you... okay with this?" Eliza asked, rattling the paper in her hand. "Since it means she's a step closer to leaving?"

He inhaled and decided to own up to the emotions churning inside of him. "Can't say I don't want to know what I need to do to keep her here." Eliza looked so shocked and worried by the statement that Mac wished he'd kept his mouth shut. "Never mind."

"Oh, no. There's no backing out of that one. You're falling in love with her. No man makes a statement like that unless he's teetering on the edge or already over it."

"Would it be so crazy if I said I was?"

"For a lot of people, no. For you," she said with the experience of someone who'd known him most of his life due to her being best friends with Marsali, "it's kind of amazing."

"Why do you say it like that?" He wasn't *unlovable*. Or difficult. Was he?

"You've dated how many women over the years—don't answer that—but you've never seemed all that interested. Nor did you seem to care much when they moved on. Until now."

"Your point?"

"Why her?" Eliza asked, her gaze piercing enough to make him want to squirm.

"Like I told Marsali, Victoria is different. She's... I can't explain it. I look at her and I think... things."

"Good things? Bad things? Or just sexual things?"

He stared at Eliza and tried again. "I *see* things. I see more. Me and her and..."

"Wow," she said, drawing out the word. "Oh, wow," she said again. "The last mighty bachelor has officially fallen. Who'da thunk it?"

He fought off the awkwardness of the conversation. "Can we be serious here?"

"What was your question again?"

He raked a hand over his head and wished V—women —were as easy to handle as a spreadsheet or business plan. Something concrete that didn't change as often as their moods or clothes. Something... that didn't want to leave.

"Mac, hey. Come on, I'm teasing."

When he met Eliza's gaze, he found himself at a loss for words. "I know. But while I'm thinking these things, she's thinking *other* things." He nodded to the sign he'd just noticed nearby about the event with V's name in oversized letters and a picture of her from her time in New York City.

"Like getting back to her old life."

He nodded.

"Okay, so here's my take on V," Eliza said. "I don't know her well, but I think she's scared and she's scrambling. I went online and watched that performance. You know, the one where she... Yeah. So *no one*—and I speak from experience here—can take that kind of public failure and walk away without some PTSD."

"It wasn't failure. She *fell*."

"We all fall in one way or another at one time or another," Eliza said, shaking her head. "V lost a lot that day. Her health, the *years* of training, her livelihood… She's literally putting herself back together like Humpty Dumpty and figuring things out a moment at a time."

"What are you saying?"

"Have you ever heard that old cliche about the only way to keep something is to let it go?"

Yeah, *not* what he wanted to hear.

Eliza's lips twisted into a wobbly line. "I hate to say it, but you can't make her stay, Mac. And you can't make her love you. Either she wants to—does—or not. But pressuring her isn't going to get what you want, that's for sure."

He pondered those words for a long moment, looking out at the lobby area and the thinning crowd of parents slowly herding kids out the door. At thirty-four, he had plenty of time left for fatherhood, but right now? Here? He pictured himself showing up to get his kid and his wife and taking them out to dinner before going home to do homework and—

"Mac, V's awesome. She really is. But maybe instead of wondering how you're going to keep her, you should ask yourself what you're going to do to make it so that she never wants to leave?"

"Kidnapping?"

Eliza wrinkled her nose. "I don't think even you can get by with a scenario like that."

"Any suggestions?"

A smile pulled at her lips. "Just be you. But I can see what I can do about making sure she feels welcome, and that involves us girls. You wouldn't happen to know her work schedule, would you?"

He pulled out his phone and the screenshot he'd made of the Reels schedule.

Eliza took a look, and Mac noted that V's class must have ended because the older kids began to emerge, dance bags slung over their shoulders and phones in hand.

A few minutes later, V shook hands with the man who'd been in class taking photographs, and he left, head down and staring at his camera as he scrolled through pictures on the way out the door.

When Mac turned back toward the classroom, he noticed V headed his way.

"Hey," she said, joining them. "What are you doing here?"

"I thought you might need a ride home," he said.

"V, it's good to see you," Eliza said. "I have to get Piper home, but I wanted to invite you to a little gathering I'm hosting for Marsali. I'd love it if you'd join us."

"Oh. Uh, I'll have to check my calendar but—"

"Tuesday night? Mac showed me your schedule—sorry, I took the liberty—but since you're off, the timing is great for me so… Please say you'll come?"

"Um, okay. Yeah, I suppose. Do I need to bring anything?" V asked, sliding him a glance before focusing on Eliza again.

"Just yourself. The rest is on me. I'll get your number from Mac later and send you the details. Now, I'm out of here," she said as she took a step back and lifted both hands to wave. "Have fun."

Eliza walked away to gather up Piper and her dance bag and Mac stared down at V.

"You know, I appreciate the offer, but doesn't a fancy

businessman like yourself have better things to do than chauffeur me around?" she asked.

He chuckled as he leaned low and kissed the top of her head since he knew he probably shouldn't let the kids see their teacher in a full-out PDA. "Nothing that can't wait. Hey, you."

"Mmm. What are you *really* doing here?"

"I wanted to make sure you ate dinner."

"Keep feeding me and I won't be able to see my feet, much less get them off the floor."

She was underweight for her height, and having recently read up on ballerinas, he knew they took their weight and company expectations very seriously, so much so many of them suffered from anorexia. He didn't get that vibe from her but knew she watched what she ate. "Are you finished for the evening?"

"I am. I have to get my stuff, though," she said, turning to retrace her steps toward the room.

"Who was the photographer?"

"Oh, um, he's from New York," she said, naming the newspaper. "He actually flew down with my mother because he pitched an idea to do a story on me, and his paper gave him the go-ahead. I agreed to do it."

"You've been meeting with him?" Jealousy reared like the big green monster it was, but he couldn't help it. Anything that pulled her back to New York wasn't something he liked.

"Yeah. Well, once—at London's Lattes. I saw Oliver and Marsali while I was there," she said, leading the way back into her classroom. "He's hung out at the bar a few times during my shift to ask questions and take a photo, and again tonight."

Mac followed her, and once inside the classroom, he

watched as she frowned down at the knotted strings of one shoe.

"Let me." He knelt beside her and managed to undo the knot, his hand around her ankle as he slipped the shoe from her foot.

She tried to pull away and he frowned.

"Dancers' feet are *ugly*," she said. "Trust me."

He held his grip and tugged, holding her gaze while he dug his thumb into her arch.

She gasped and then groaned, her eyelashes fluttering. "Oh my… *Ohhh*."

A laugh left his chest at her very vocal and appealing response. He watched her closely, thoroughly enamored with the way she tilted her head back and closed her eyes, hands gripping the chair until her knuckles turned white. "Good?"

She bit her lower lip and nodded, seemingly unable to do more.

Make her want to never leave. Wasn't that what Eliza had said?

He settled himself on the floor in front of her, released her ankle, and used both thumbs to work some magic. "I give a really good massage, you know."

"D-do you?"

Chapter 20

Who knew? V thought later as she sat beside Mac on a swing near Carolina Cove's pier.

After a thorough foot and calf massage, Mac had taken her out to eat at a local Italian place. She'd gotten a salad but agreed to try one of Mac's decadent mushroom raviolis. He'd offered her more, but she refused, knowing every bite meant more training time in the studio.

Her class had gone well tonight. Amazingly so considering it was the first one she'd had teaching the advanced kids. The routine was perfect and designed to showcase the students' individual talents and strengths.

When V had shown up that evening, Mrs. Taylor asked if she would take over the advanced routine for the spring student program—in a matter of days—due to a death in the instructor's family.

V had hesitated for a long moment, completely taken aback. But Mrs. Taylor had assured V the students were competent. One class and she would see their potential.

V had made a few suggestions this evening and talked to them about their nerves in performing in front of a crowd. Normally they'd dance at a local elementary school, but this year the program was taking place in downtown Wilmington at the arts center.

Mrs. Taylor's second request that V actually join the program and dance something of her choosing gave her pause, but she'd accepted the invitation. Given how well her workouts and training had gone, she saw no reason to say no. Especially when the woman had been so kind to V in allowing her to use the studio without charging her.

"Hey. Where'd you go?"

The softly posed question drew her attention back to the man sitting beside her, and she curled up against his side, welcoming the heat generated by his big body.

Mac wrapped an arm around her and she leaned her head against his shoulder. "Just thinking about the program."

"If you're not up for it—"

"I am."

Mac's head tilted in her direction and she smiled up at him. "You look worried."

"Only because a few weeks ago you were in some serious pain. I was surprised to walk in tonight and see your name on the billing posters."

"All dancers have pain. And I was surprised, too, considering Mrs. Taylor didn't mess around and had them done *today* once I'd agreed this morning. Apparently, she'd already had them designed, hoping I'd say yes, and just had to give the green light to the printers. But it's good," she said with a nod. "It'll be a great way to get video of my performance to send to my company so they can see I'm getting back to normal."

When he remained silent, she braced a hand against his chest and pushed herself upright, facing him on the swing. "Mac?"

"I want you to be happy, Victoria. But don't expect me to like it if that means you leave."

She bit her lip and then leaned into him, sliding her hands up his chest to gently tug his head low for a kiss that was sweet and slow and lingering.

Mac gathered her up and shifted her weight so that she sat on his lap, cuddled against him as the kissing continued. Seeing as how they were in public with the boardwalk directly behind them, they couldn't do more than kiss, and after a last nuzzling brush of his mouth against hers, Mac tucked her head under his chin and set the swing in motion.

V closed her eyes, never remembering a moment when she'd ever felt such comfort, such safety and warmth and lo—

She froze, tensed against him and the thought springing into her head. Because it wasn't true. Couldn't be. She hadn't known Mac long enough to feel anything more than simple friendship and… maybe more than a little fascination. Attraction. Right?

But if it was more, what did it mean? With her future in New York and his here… Oh, no. No, no, no.

"What's wrong? Are you cold?" he asked, his arms around her, smoothing up and down her back as though to fight off the cool breeze.

"No, I'm… I'm tired. I think I should get home—I mean back. To Vic's. You know what I mean."

She was aware of Mac's gaze on her, narrowing with every stumbling word she said and her sudden change of mood.

"Okay."

She flashed him a smile and swung her legs off the swing and down to hop off his lap.

"Careful."

"I'm fine." The words held more than a bit of snap to them and she winced. "I mean… Mac, I'm healed. Okay? I haven't had real pain in a while, and there's no need to treat me like I'll shatter if I get up from a swing."

"A couple of weeks is not a while, and I just didn't want you to stumble."

She crossed her arms over her front and backed up until her legs hit the low railing behind her and she couldn't go any farther. "Right. Fine."

She knew she was overreacting. She knew *he knew* she was overreacting, and his gaze said it all, but she couldn't help herself. Not when her thoughts had slid into the *L word* zone without her permission.

She'd worried about Mac being the type of guy to get attached while they dated, but now as she marched her way to his SUV, she had to wonder about herself.

Mac was quiet the entire drive to Vic's condo. She was just as silent, staring out the window at the little seaside town that had so quickly become home.

Home. She'd thought it again.

When had *that* happened?

The *L* word thought wasn't the only blunder she'd made tonight, and she'd referenced Vic's as *home* when *home* was in NYC, in the tiny apartment she shared with other dancers. It wasn't here. It wasn't *this*. This life wasn't her life.

Her life wasn't *this*.

Mac pulled up beneath the canopied entrance and she grabbed her bag. "I'm tired. I'll… text you later. Or tomorrow. Good night, Mac." She leaned over and kissed him but didn't allow herself to linger. She grabbed the handle and hopped out of the vehicle, rushing into the building like Baryshnikov stood on the other side waiting to partner with her.

She slogged through the lobby toward the elevator and rode up with an older couple and their freaky-faced little mutt. The dog glared at V with its beady eyes, and V couldn't help but think the dog picked up on her mood since pets generally liked her. By the time the elevator stopped at her floor, the dog bared teeth and V was ready to growl back.

Finally she stuck her key into the lock and walked in to find her parents slow-dancing to Etta James's "*At Last*." No freaking way. "Uh."

"Come in, come in," her mother said, beaming at V. "We've been waiting for you to get home."

V silently growled.

"Look."

Her mother stuck out her left hand, and V choked on the rock gleaming at her like a flashlight. "Come again?"

Vic whispered something only her mother could hear, and Amy giggled and blushed. *Oh, I so don't want to know what that was about.* "You're engaged?"

"No. We're *married!*"

Married? "Married, married?"

"Yeah," Vic said, beaming as he hugged Amy. "I'm so glad you came to visit, Tori. If you hadn't, your mother wouldn't have followed, and we wouldn't be together now. Thank you."

"*Married*, married?" she asked again, unable to take it in. Amy laughed and moved toward V, arms open. Amy hugged V close, and V stared at her father, feeling like she'd entered some sort of alternate universe. "For real? This isn't some late April Fool's joke?"

"Nope. All real. Isn't it wonderful?"

Amy finally released her and V stepped back to take a good look. Yeah, that rock definitely looked real. "So you're... moving here?"

"Of course! You know how much I've hated New York winters since Steve died. Are you happy for us?"

V forced her reservations aside since they didn't matter now that the ink was drying on the wedding certificate and nodded. "Of course! I'm just… I'm going to miss looking out and not seeing you in the audience."

"What? What do you mean?" Vic asked, his bushy eyebrows lowering.

"Well, for one, Mrs. Taylor has asked me to perform in the spring recital."

"Oh. Oh, honey, are you sure you're up for it?"

"Yes, Mom, I am. And I decided I'm going to do my solo. The one I danced last in New York."

Chapter 21

Mac ranted silently as he pummeled the heavyweight bag in front of him.

"You got anyone in particular in mind as you do that, or just the state of the world in general?"

Mac turned to find his best friend and future brother-in-law standing several feet away, Denz the bodyguard beside him. "State of the world," he said, the words emerging more than a bit glum.

Oliver moved close and took position behind the bag, holding it. "Does this have anything to do with a certain tiny ballet dancer?"

Mac hauled off and hit the bag without thought, the sound echoing off the wall beside them. "She's dancing at the recital. The one Piper's in that we all got invited to."

"You're upset because a professional dancer is dancing?"

Mac took position and began pummeling the bag again. "I'm upset because of what it means."

When Oliver blinked at him, Mac groaned. "She's going back to New York soon."

"Ah."

Ah? That's it? That's all Oliver had to say? "Do you know anything about the reporter who's here, interviewing her?"

"Yeah. I checked into him."

Mac waited and Oliver grinned, drawing out the torturous moment.

"He's legit. Does arts and entertainment pieces."

"He's going to be there. I think she's hoping he'll watch her dance and talk about her comeback."

"Isn't that what she's always planned? Ah," Oliver drawled.

"Don't say it," Mac ordered. "Yes, I knew from the beginning that she planned to leave. I just—"

"Hoped she'd fall so head-over-heels in love with you she'd change her mind like in one of those Hallmark movies?"

"You walked away," Mac countered. "You left Hollywood and chose the girl." Mac lowered his gloved hands and stalked away, unable to believe how petulant and pathetic he sounded.

He was a grown man who'd fallen in love with a grown woman—one who'd worked hard to achieve all that she had. Who'd sacrificed and literally bled for her career. Who did he think he was to believe she would give all of that up for him?

"So leave Carolina Cove," Oliver said. "Choose the girl."

"What?"

"You might like New York if you tried. It's not *that* bad. Right, Denz?"

AN HOUR LATER, Mac stalked into Reels, his long strides eating up the distance. V had texted and said she would be at the studio practicing her solo since she didn't have time to do so on the nights she taught there.

Mac knocked on the door to the office and opened it when Vic's deep voice boomed out to enter. Mac walked in, surprised to find Victoria's mother in the process of getting off Vic's lap. "Uhhh. Sorry."

"Shut it and come on in, Boss Man. Oh, and meet the new Mrs."

"Mrs.?" He shifted his gaze from Vic to a beaming Amy. "You remarried?"

"We did. Just goes to show you that it's never too late to mend broken fences. What's up?" Vic asked.

He looked at the two of them and decided he didn't have the energy to ask how it had come about so quickly or what V's take on it was. "I wanted to talk to you. About your daughter. Did you know she's dancing in the upcoming recital?"

"She told us last night," Amy said. "I worry about her doing that solo. Especially after what happened last time."

"Wait… you mean she's dancing the same dance she was doing when she—"

"That's the one," Vic said. "She told us after she got home from her dinner with you. She didn't mention it?"

"Not that she planned to do the same one, no." The news hit like a punch to the gut. The dance contained a long series of jumps and spins at impossible speeds. He'd watched other videos online, demonstrations of dancers who'd performed the same sequence without incident. But after making the landing that had shattered V's leg the last time, they went on to do yet another round of spins "Do you think she can do it?"

The three of them exchanged glances and Vic sat back in his chair.

"I think she has to find that out for herself. For good or for bad. Anything we say to try to stop her will only make her more determined to prove us wrong."

Mac nodded, knowing it was true. V had proven to be stubborn, determined—and he liked her that way. He just wished her determination didn't come at such a cost.

More was at risk with this dance than ever.

Chapter 22

V showered and changed after her time at the studio, worked at the bar during the early afternoon and evening, and then headed out to meet the girls for GNO.

Apparently the party was one of several upcoming gatherings planned as part of the wedding frenzy, but this one only included the close-knit group of friends.

V was surprised to find herself included in the mix but then figured it had more to do with the fact she dated Mac. Maybe he'd put them up to asking her?

Either way, she was extremely touched by the inclusion, especially after discovering just how intimate the gathering was.

"Grab a drink," Eliza ordered as V made her way through the gorgeous oceanfront beach house. "Whose home is this?"

"One of Oliver's movie buddies. They're going to be using it for a set, and Amelia asked if we could hang out a few hours. The hors d'oeuvres are there, drinks there, and the view is… there," Eliza said with a wave of her hand to indicate the expansive view of the Atlantic Ocean outside.

Dusk was setting in the beautiful windows that had been shoved back, allowing the sound of the surf and the breeze to filter in. "Beautiful."

"Isn't it, though? Come on, the other girls went on a tour, so let's go find them."

Amelia, Marsali, Amelia's best friend, Izzy, were all upstairs. Eliza and V joined them, taking in the beautifully decorated bedrooms, bathrooms with tubs that made her want to strip and crawl in immediately, and closets that were bigger than the entire apartment she'd shared back in New York. "Wow."

"Right?" Marsali said from beside her. "I think if we hid well enough, we could stay and they'd never know we were here."

V watched as Eliza held out her hand, and Amelia pulled a dollar from her pocket and handed it over. "What's that for?"

"Amelia bet me it would take *two* drinks before Marse would start tipsy-talking."

"And your guess?" V asked, smiling.

"Not even one," Eliza said with a wink. "My girl is *lightweight*."

"Certified," Marsali said, attempting to high-five her friend and missing terribly.

Everyone laughed at the sight and turned to make their way downstairs, careful to keep track of Marsali's progress.

"V, I'm so glad you joined us," Marsali said. "You're such a great addition to our little group."

"And it doesn't leave me feeling like the odd man out since all of these guys are married or engaged," Izzy stated, her straight blond hair sliding over her bare shoulder.

V noted that the ladies had all dressed casually for the evening, though each had their own distinctive style. Izzy's outfit was a flowing boho top and skinny jeans, Marsali wore a matching summer suit with cropped jacket and ankle pants, while Eliza and Amelia both wore dresses like the black wrap dress V had chosen, the same dress she'd worn on her first date with Mac since it was the only one she'd brought with her.

"V, you look impossibly tiny. We're the same height but I'd kill for your figure," Izzy stated.

"No doubt we'd all have it if we worked out and trained as hard as she does," Amelia said, leading the way to the kitchen, where the waterfall island held an assortment of delectable-looking treats.

"Come on, girls, dig in!" Eliza said.

Everyone gathered plates and utensils and napkins, and V's mouth watered at the sight and smell of some of the nibbles. She took one of the small plates to make the rounds, eyeing each one closely since she tended to make times like these worth the price in the gym and studio later.

"So she does eat," Izzy murmured.

V looked up and found all of the women just standing there watching her. "I do," she said with a grin. "Special occasions are my favorite splurges."

The group settled down at the table with plates and drinks and laughter. They oohed and ahhed over certain nibbles and discussed their week so far, and V loved the companionship and friendship offered as complaints were met with encouragement and suggestions, and celebrations were cheered.

"So, V," Eliza said. "We're all dying to know. What's happening with you and Mac?"

"Oh, give her a break," Izzy said. "No one likes that kind of spotlight."

"Uh-uh. She's one of us and sharing is caring," Eliza

said again, head tilted and inquisitive smile in place on her beautiful face. "So? What's happening?"

Every eye turned toward her and V gripped her drink a little tighter. "Um… Well, we're friends."

Silence followed her statement and it took some doing to meet and maintain their gazes.

"That's it?" Eliza asked.

"Yes. That's it. I'm going back to New York. Soon," she stressed. "We… can't exactly be more than friends."

V found herself faltering, especially when she viewed the disappointment etched in their various expressions. "Don't get me wrong, Mac is wonderful. He's smart and handsome and—"

"Sexy," Eliza stated. "What?" she asked of Marsali. "I've been friends with the man as long as I've been friends with you. I'm allowed to notice."

V smiled at the best-friend banter and nodded. "He *is* sexy. Very sexy," she added.

"So you do feel chemistry?" Marsali asked.

While the women nibbled and drank and contemplated her love life, V struggled to find the words. "There is definitely chemistry. But knowing I won't be here for much longer, we've… kept it in check. Unlike most dancers' reputations, I'm not the type to sleep around, especially when I know our relationship will end."

"Will it? Does it have to? Mac is a businessman," Marsali said. "He travels."

"To New York City?"

"He… I'm just saying it wouldn't *have* to be the end. Only if you wanted it to."

"That might be true… if Mac feels the same way— which he hasn't said he does… So it's kind of a moot point, wouldn't you say?"

"V—"

"He's a good guy. I don't want to hurt him."

More than one gasp filled the air, and V knew, in saying the simple statement, she'd just owned up to the fact there was more than chemistry at stake.

"You think he's… falling in love?" Marsali asked. "Are *you?*"

V plucked at an imaginary piece of lint on her dress and stared into the depths of her glass. "I think it doesn't matter when my life is elsewhere. I warned you when you asked me to be part of your database that I didn't intend to stay. My goals—my dreams—are in New York."

"Dreams change, V," Eliza said, lifting her glass for a sip. "Every single day, dreams change. They grow and morph into new ones we didn't know we even desired until… we just do."

"Babies for me," Amelia said softly. "Twenty years ago, Lincoln wanted to settle down and have babies, and I wanted no part of it. My dream was to be free. But now? Oh, how that dream has changed." She smoothed a hand over her flat stomach and smiled. "This little one is a dream come true now. What about you, Eliza? Izzy?"

"My dream has always been to celebrate the moments that make us who we are," Eliza said. "James—ex boyfriend and business partner," she said to V, "almost took that from me, but Carter proved to me that people make mistakes and they learn from them and… we move forward. Always forward."

"I'm still a work in progress," Izzy stated, plopping a chocolate into her mouth to chew. "Being an artist means learning to go with the flow but capitalizing on it when it happens. I guess my dream at this point would be to work my art into a viable future that pays the bills more than they do at this point."

"My business and dream and life go hand-in-hand,"

Marsali said. "I love matching people up, but now Oliver and I… My dream is to be the happy—not perfect, but *happy*," she clarified, "couple I know we can be if we both work at making it happen. It's hard, especially when our ideals and brands didn't line up. Breaking up with him was the hardest thing I've ever done—"

"Wait, you broke up with Oliver Beck?" V asked, frowning. "When was this?"

"Around Valentine's Day of all times," Marsali said, rolling her eyes. "He'd been offered this huge role in a series that meant taking it *all* off and doing… Well, I couldn't deal. I love him, but that wasn't something I was okay with. Thankfully, Oliver came to his senses."

"And fired his agent," Eliza added.

"The point is," Marsali said, "dreams and plans change and adjust over time. They have to when people enter our lives or something happens to change our course. It's up to us to recognize a good change and adjust our sails to go with the new direction."

V pondered the quietly spoken words. Did she know the difference between good change and bad?

Chapter 23

Several days had passed since V had gone to the all-girls gathering, and as Mac entered Reels, he couldn't help but think something had been said that night to skew V's feelings toward him—and not in a good way.

Ever since that night, she had been quiet, a little withdrawn. Not her usual smiling and vivacious self. But that GNO had taken place after their conversation on the swing, and that night had ended strangely so... maybe it was the two combined?

Especially considering she was also now working the equivalent of three jobs. Bartending, training the older kids at the dance studio, *and* training for hours on end every day herself.

He waited for his eyes to adjust to the darker interior of the building after being outside. The moment they did, he found himself looking at V working the bar as effortlessly as she danced.

Seeing her the other night with the kids had left him wondering, and he'd done some research. Research he hoped would give her some pause before simply leaving Carolina Cove and him behind. "Good afternoon."

He made his way behind the bar and, after a quick glance around to make sure no one was paying them any attention, stole a kiss from her luscious lips.

"Hey. What are you doing here?"

"Well, I started thinking and realized I need more behind-the-scenes training. Bar, restaurant, what have you. You interested in showing me the ropes?"

She frowned at him. "You're going to bus tables?"

"Possibly. Every good businessman knows exactly how his business works and what it takes to run it, as well as what each key component does to keep the process working. So, yeah, I intend to be back in the kitchen, up front with the waitstaff—but I'm starting with the bar."

"And you just so happened to pick the day I'm working to do this?"

He leaned his head low and stole another kiss from the smile curling her lips up. "I may have ulterior motives in mind." He wanted to spend more time with her, especially if she planned to leave soon. Maybe he was just rubbing salt into the wound, but it was his wound to salt like a margarita glass.

And if all else failed, there was alcohol nearby to add to the salt. And limes.

"Okay. Well, this is the slow time of day, but it'll get busy fast and we have to be ready. Prepping is everything." She paused. "You're sure you want to do this?"

"I'm sure." Because short of kidnapping her, he couldn't think of another way to spend time with her. V's availability had become increasingly limited. When she wasn't teaching or bartending, she was training for her own dance, and so exhausted by the end of the day she didn't have the energy to do much.

She found a knife, tossed it into the air, and caught it before flipping it around to hand to him. "You're on chop duty."

Mac set to work slicing lemons and limes while V replenished supplies like the salt in the container used for rimming glasses. The irony wasn't lost on him. "What are you doing after your shift?"

She paused and leaned her slight body against the counter.

"Training. And I scheduled an extra class tonight. I'm sorry."

An extra class. On top of the others *and* the training? He eyed her tiny body, wondering how close she was to maxing out. She was an athlete, no doubt about it, but even she had to have a cap. "I know how important the recital is to you."

"It is. Mrs. Taylor has given me a lot of leeway with the class that I have, and they're good. Like really good. I've challenged them to up their performance, but it takes practice and dedication."

"And after that you're training," he said. "Can I give you a ride home?" He didn't like the thought of her wandering the streets, walking home in the dark, especially when she'd be tired and weaker than normal.

"I'd… That'd be great. Mom and Vic are going to New York after the recital to move my mom back here. I'll have Vic's truck to use then, though I may be safer walking. It's been a while since I've driven anything. I just keep my license current as a form of ID."

He honestly couldn't imagine living in a place where he never got to drive, to go out on a beautiful day and have the wind in his hair. Take a drive out on the sand to an isolated spot and just breathe.

She headed toward him to go back into the kitchen,

and he quickly turned and blocked her way, one hand on either side of the walkway. "You have to pay the toll."

V's expression softened and she placed her hands on his stomach and balanced herself as she rose onto her toes in that way ballet dancers had, just to bring her mouth closer to his. Even then he had to lower his head and bend his knees, but he loved it when she leaned her head back on her neck and gazed up at him, brushed her lips across his, leaving a bit of raspberry-flavored lip gloss behind.

"Toll paid," she said softly. "Now let me by before my boss fires me."

"He won't do that."

"No? I'm not so sure."

"He'd fire your boss's boss if that ever happened."

"Oh, that guy."

"Yeah, that guy. How do you feel about that guy?"

Mac was aware of the panic in V's gaze before she sucked in a breath and managed to duck by him, leaving the question unanswered.

But then, wasn't that an answer?

Chapter 24

V took the day of the recital off. She tried to sleep in and couldn't, her body too aware of the day's importance and unable to be fooled.

She ate well, making sure she had fuel for energy, and she stretched periodically throughout the day. And she prayed, something she hadn't done for a very long time.

It couldn't hurt, though, and she knew there had to be a reason she'd been through what she had. Maybe it was to bring her parents back together? She wouldn't have thought it possible, but they seemed happy, happier than she'd ever known either of them to be individually.

Maybe her injury had occurred so that she would take a step back and realize just how important it was to be a part of a world bigger than herself and her career and her wants.

Had she not come here, she wouldn't have known about her father's heart attack or the extent of his medical debt. Wouldn't have met Mac and her wide assortment of friends.

If nothing else, her talk with the ladies the other night

had pinpointed that for V. That each of them, in some way, was meant to influence the other. To help. Aid. Cheer the other on. Remove one and—

She sucked in a sharp breath, only then realizing *she* was the one determined to remove herself. She had no doubt the group would go on as friendly and cheerful as they were now, but they had made a point of inviting her, including her, and *she* would be the one missing. The one missing out due to distance and choices—

"Breathe," Mrs. Taylor said.

V turned to find the older woman regarding her with a worried glance.

"Are you all right, my dear?"

"Yes. Fine."

The woman's gaze narrowed shrewdly and V swallowed. Hard. "I just… There is a lot riding on this." Because for some reason she couldn't fathom at the time, V had invited Jonathan Frakkes to stay and witness her attempt to dance the dance that had tried to destroy her.

Perspectives being what they were, she couldn't help but wonder at the whys when, to accomplish her dream and meet her goals, a part of her would have to be ripped away. Pain had driven her here. But to go back, she'd feel pain again. Different, but all the more hurtful.

"More than I think you understand," the woman said.

"What do you mean?"

"This dance of yours is about more than proving to those watching that you can do it. It's about you, dancing to the best of your ability, and being able to accept it for whatever that ability is. Ahhh, you don't like that. Your expression gives you away, my dear."

"I won't make it in New York if I can't regain the level I was on. If I can't exceed it."

Mrs. Taylor patted V's hand and nodded.

"Trust me, my dear, you won't make it if you can't accept yourself either way. *That* is the key. Now, I'm sure you have a guest or two waiting, so I'll leave you to it. The students are prepping in the holding areas."

"I'll be out soon."

Mrs. Taylor left the dressing room located at the back of the beautiful arts center where the recital would take place, and V heard her speaking to someone outside.

V sucked in a breath and finished her eye makeup, checked her lipstick one last time, aware of the door opening after a short knock.

"Tori? You decent?"

"Yeah, Dad, come on in," she said, turning on the chair to see her parents entering. Her mother carried a bouquet of flowers, and her father looked uncomfortable in his suit. "You dressed up for me? Looking snazzy, Vic."

Vic tugged at his tie and managed a smile.

"Only because your mother made me. I didn't even wear a suit to our wedding."

"Well, you look fabulous," she said, standing to hug them both while being careful of her makeup.

"Look at you," Vic said, taking in V's costume. "Baby, you look beautiful."

"Thank you."

"Oh, these are for you," Amy said, handing over the flowers.

"They're gorgeous, Mom. Thank you."

"I asked Mac if I could give you mine first. Wait until you see the bouquet he's brought you," Amy said, visibly aflutter.

"He's here? Outside?"

"I think he wants some time alone with you," Vic said. "Your friends are coming tonight, too, aren't they?"

She nodded, noting her father had said *your friends*

rather than *Mac's friends*. Maybe she was making something out of nothing, but she liked the distinction. Marsali, Eliza, Amelia, and Izzy *were* her friends. Friends she would miss once—

The hot sprinkle of tears was a sure sign she needed to shift her focus. Getting emotional now would not only cause her delays since she'd have to repair her makeup but also serve to distract her from the goal she'd set for the evening. She couldn't lose focus. Couldn't do anything but breathe and dance and nail every single movement. "Thank you for the flowers, and for coming."

"Of course. We wouldn't be anywhere else. Vic? Honey, we should go."

Vic lingered despite her mother's hand on his arm urging him to follow, and before she knew it, V was on the receiving end of one of her father's bear hugs.

"*Don't* break a leg," he whispered.

V laughed at the awful joke and nodded. "I'll do my best not to."

Her parents left the room and V stayed where she was, facing the door. A second later, Mac's tall, broad-shouldered form filled the space, and she sucked in a breath. Wow. Her mother wasn't kidding when she said Mac had brought flowers. The bouquet took both his massive hands to hold. "Did you leave any at the florist?"

He smiled at the teasing.

"Not many."

His gaze swept over her and she felt her entire body warm in the looking. Maybe because the look packed so much heat. He'd never seen her in costume before, and as he took in every detail, she lifted her chin and reveled in the admiration she saw.

She stepped forward and lowered her head to smell the mix of roses and eucalyptus, jasmine and more.

"You're absolutely stunning, Victoria."

"Thank you."

"I mean it. But then you're always stunning."

She set the bouquet aside and moved toward him, sliding her hands up his chest. His wrapped around her rib cage, and she shivered at the difference in their size, his strength, when he gently lifted her up.

"I want to kiss you but I don't want to muss your lipstick."

"I've always preferred a man who'd ruin my lipstick rather than my mascara," she said.

She slid her hands around the nape of his neck and tugged him low, kissing him because lipstick could always be fixed.

By the time Mac let her up for air, she'd almost forgotten her nerves, but the increasing sound of chatter and music and anticipation from outside her dressing room left her very aware the clock was ticking. "I have to go. My group goes on first so that I can warm up while all of the other classes perform."

Mac nodded and kissed her again, looking adorable with the red smudges on his lips.

"Read the card," he murmured before he kissed her once more, quickly. "And don't forget to fix your lipstick."

Mac exited the room and she turned toward the mirror lined with bright lights. Once she'd repaired the damage, she turned to the massive bouquet and dug until she found the card tucked within the stems.

Dance like nobody's watching. Love, Mac

She blinked away tears, a huff of air leaving her chest that she couldn't seem to replace.

Love?

Chapter 25

Mrs. Taylor had neglected to say that, in addition to Jonathan Frakkes, there were local news crews in attendance, but the flash of the camera lenses had given them away as she approached the stage.

She waited in the wings, giving the children time to settle into the audience wherever they could, because Mrs. Taylor wanted them to see why they practiced and worked so hard, why they came to class and skipped extra desserts, and how doing so meant achieving and learning a craft and skill that belonged to few with the perseverance to see it through.

V closed her eyes, took a breath. Waiting for that first strain of violin to begin. Once it did... every inhalation, every step, every ounce of willpower and determination and fear fueled her movements and added height, depth, emotion. Adrenaline pulsed through her body as she flew across the stage, the music calling to her very soul as she lost herself in the notes.

When it was over, she realized she didn't actually

remember the individual movements, not the nuances. Only the start and the rush and now the end.

Instinct told her that her timing had been impeccable, and she didn't need to watch a recording to know she had performed every movement close to if not perfectly.

She'd done it. She'd actually done it.

She had conquered the routine that had nearly destroyed her.

The silence that followed reinforced her thoughts more than the standing ovation. She'd touched her audience in a way that left them struggling for words, just as she struggled for breath as she took her bows.

Quite a few of the students flew on stage, bringing her flowers until V couldn't hold them all. As a group, they posed for photos, and V battled tears when her older students came to hug her and she saw several of them crying.

They had the dream. And she knew from experience that they'd just pictured themselves in her as she had as a child watching her favorite ballerinas take the stage by storm.

The thunderous applause led V to urge the children to take another bow before she did the same. Then all clapped when Mrs. Taylor made her way on stage, and V gave the woman the bouquet in her arms, hugging her and thanking her through the tight vise of tears.

Once that was done, V helped Mrs. Taylor get the kids off stage to gather bags and their own little plastic-wrapped flowers. It was then that V noticed the ache.

Not unexpected but unwelcome all the same.

V held her head high and ignored the pain beginning to take hold of her body. She made her way to stand beside Mrs. Taylor and greeted the parents and praised their children, encouraging them to stick with it.

Many of the students still danced, their excitement too much to contain. Others gathered bags and flowers, ready to move on to special dinners or whatever would happen next.

A few of the parents stopped to ask V questions, hinting at one-on-one training classes so their child could advance more rapidly than the general classes provided. V hedged in her answers, not discouraging the training but not agreeing to tutoring given her hopes of returning to New York.

"Well, how does it feel to conquer your demon, Ms. Valentine?"

She turned her head and spotted Jonathan Frakkes nearby, phone up and at the ready. "It feels *wonderful.*"

She watched as Jonathan moved closer and braced herself for whatever he might say about her performance.

"So what happens now?"

She inhaled and smiled at the man. "Now I wait," she said honestly.

"But you're hoping this will prompt invitations to return to your company? Or to another?" he asked, still recording.

"Absolutely."

"I will say that I was thoroughly impressed. I… feared another fall and held my breath during that bit."

She forced a laugh. "I guess it proves dancers can be knocked down, but the important thing is that they get back up."

"And now I think I have my quote. Thank you, Ms. Valentine," he said, ending the recording. "I have a plane to catch, but I'll be sure to adhere to our agreement and send you a copy of my article before it hits the public."

"Thank you."

"It was a pleasure watching your comeback," he said,

taking hold of her hand to shake gently before lifting it to his lips to kiss. "Now if you'll excuse me…"

V held her mask in place while Jonathan walked away, before she turned toward the group of adults now gathered backstage smiling in her direction.

"V… Oh, my gosh, girlfriend," Marsali said. "I'm *speechless*. I'm just… That was unbelievable!"

"You were wonderful," Oliver added with a nod.

The others chimed in with their praises, and she accepted them and the hugs and flowers that they presented her with.

She was aware that Mac stood back from the rest, watched her every move, and that his gaze was far too discerning for her comfort.

"Please go change and come to dinner with us," Marsali said. "We're going to Seventh Heaven."

"Oh, I don't know. I'd need to shower and get this makeup off first."

"Go. We'll get a table and wait for you. Mac can escort you," Marsali said. "Please? We have to celebrate this!"

Knowing she couldn't refuse, she nodded. "Okay, but don't blame me when I'm late. Stage makeup is a far cry from regular makeup."

She watched as the group left the backstage area and smiled in Mac's direction while ignoring his gaze as she walked into her private dressing room, carrying flowers with her. "Would you mind taking some of these to your car while I get ready? I wasn't expecting so man—"

"How much pain are you in right now?"

She turned, careful to keep the mask in place when she wanted to crumple and howl. Instead she leaned her hips against her dressing table to take the weight off her leg. "I'm on top of the world. Don't ruin it."

"Victoria—"

"I'm on top of the freaking world," she said, blinking hard and fast to rid herself of the instant tears that threatened to escape as pain stole her ability to breathe.

He saw too much. She knew he saw too much, and right now she needed this moment of triumph. To hold on to it as long as possible despite the pain throbbing throughout her leg and hip.

Her dance performance had been spectacular. She'd done it! Now he was going to ruin this for her?

"I'll text the gang, tell them we aren't coming."

"I'm going."

"V, I can tell you're in pain. I can see it from here."

Pain didn't begin to describe the pulsating jabs now plaguing her. "There isn't a dancer in the world who performs pain-free."

Mac grimaced and she knew she fought a battle bigger than her leg at the moment. "I will *not* give up. I will live my life and go on because I have to, don't you see?"

"You don't have to put yourself through *this*," he said, lifting a hand to indicate her leg.

"Yes, I do. I've fought too hard to be able to do what I did tonight. To *dance*." She tossed the beautiful flowers aside and used both hands to indicate the stage beyond the door. "Did you *see* that? I did it! They said I would never dance again, but I did and it was *flawless*."

"You did do it," Mac said quietly, slowly moving toward her. "And it was flawless," he agreed. "You were amazing. And now that the adrenaline is fading, you can barely take a step without limping. You're hiding the pain as best you can, but it's getting worse by the minute and… my guess is that it's really starting to take hold, isn't it?"

She refused to answer. To acknowledge his words because if she did—

"Victoria—"

"V," she corrected tightly, not liking the way her name sounded when he said it how he'd said it just now.

"How long can you do it?" he asked next, his gaze too shrewd as he studied her like a bug under a microscope. "Let's say because of this, you get your position back within your dance company. How long will you be able to keep it? This was one performance, not a full ballet. You're going to do this day after day? Night after night? How long do you think you'll be able to keep up? A few months? A year?"

"Why are you saying these things?" She shook her head, the excruciating pain making her entire body hurt to the point she wanted to curl into a ball reminiscent of her last New York performance. "Why are you being so mean?" she asked, her voice breaking.

"Ah, sweetheart, I'm just trying to get you to see what I see. It's killing me to not be able to help you right now. To know you're hurting."

"You don't know ballet. You don't *know*—"

"I know enough. More importantly I know from a business standpoint that you're a hard sell. Comeback or no."

She sucked in a breath, unable to believe he'd stand there and just—

"And even though you hate me right now for being so brutally honest with you, I'm trying to get you to see your future from a realistic viewpoint."

"You just don't want me to leave Carolina Cove."

"No, I don't. But that's not why I'm being so brutally truthful. Victoria, you deserve to dance for as long as you want to. All right? You've put in the time, the effort. Everything. But punishing your body this way for brief moments on stage will... It'll impact your longevity. I know you know that."

"You're not a doctor. Why am I even listening to you?"

But she was listening. She couldn't help but listen, because to escape the pain shredding her body, she had to focus on something and that something was Mac. On his words.

"Sweetheart, you can't dance in that kind of pain," he said, indicating her leg. "You know it's true."

She released a frustrated sound, a mix of fury and unwanted acknowledgment that he might be… No. No, no, no. He couldn't be right! "What is it with men? Huh? My ex couldn't stand it when I lost my status as a dancer. Now here you are complaining that I am! Who do you think you are?"

"I'm the man who loves you enough to tell you the truth."

"The truth?" she asked, gasping at his words. At the *L* word he'd so boldly said.

"Yes, the truth. You can't do this long-term," he said, stalking across the room to the cooler he'd apparently just noticed. "I'm not even sure you can do this short-term."

Mac flipped the lid and shook his head at the multiple ice packs inside.

Couldn't she at least get credit for planning ahead? For knowing there would be some pain and…

She couldn't— God help her, she couldn't breathe. Not when her body was riddled with tension and agony, both physical and emotional.

Mac grabbed several of the ice packs and wrapped them in towels she'd also thought to bring and then snagged her around the waist, lifting her up and carrying her vertically across the floor. He set her down next to the love seat and lifted her leg to the cushions.

"I won't stand by and watch you hurt yourself to the point you can't dance at all—or walk—with or without a cane. I just… can't."

She watched as he placed the ice packs all up and

down her leg, and it took several long moments before the cold helped ease the pain enough for her heartbeat to slow. For her body to cool and go a bit numb.

"You don't like what I'm saying, but at this point, it has to be said. You need to think ahead, Victoria," Mac continued, lowering his voice to a gentler tone. "To plan ahead. Long-term. Can you *realistically* dance a full year? Five years? Ten? What happens then? Careers ebb and flow, but I imagine dancers only have a prime number of them before they *have* to move on in some way. Am I right?"

She heard his words and knew they came from a place of concern, but she couldn't... "So now I'm beyond my prime years," she drawled, unwilling—unable—to look at him. To see the truth she felt all the way to her soul. "You have been holding back, haven't you?"

Mac swiped a hand over his face and rubbed hard.

"Do you," he said softly, "have a plan for whatever happens the day you wake up and realize your body won't do what it did on that stage?"

She stared down at the ice packs, anger and exhaustion and pain clouding her every thought. "I did... but then you ruined it when you bought out my dad," she said, her tone more than a little testy. "Mac, you need to leave."

"Victoria—"

"You've said what you obviously needed to say. I get it. You don't approve. I hear you loud and clear. Now I'm asking you to leave."

Mac stood with a soft mutter, hands fisted at his sides. After a tense moment staring down at her, he headed toward the door, where he paused again.

"I love you, Victoria. I don't expect you to say it back, but it's how I feel and you should know. I love you, and believe it or not, I want what's best for you."

She focused on the wall in front of her rather than the

man currently leaving her life. On the pain she felt not from her leg but from her heart shattering. "I love ballet and I want people in my life who support my goals and dreams, not those who spew negativity disguised as *love*."

Mac yanked open the partially closed door.

"Have it your way then."

Chapter 26

On his way out of the building, Mac texted Marsali to say they wouldn't be joining them.

He knew a barrage of questions would fly at him once Marsali checked her phone, but for now that's all he said.

"How bad is she?"

Mac turned to see Vic and Amy standing a little ways from V's dressing room door, realizing they'd probably heard every word that had been said inside. "Bad."

Vic muttered a soft curse, and Amy patted the man's arm, silent tears rolling down her cheeks.

"I knew it," Vic said softly. "I knew she shouldn't risk it. If she keeps it up, she could shatter that leg again and all those bolts and pins—"

His voice broke and Mac felt the same level of frustrated anger. But what could he do? V was an adult. One with the right to make her own decisions. Whether he agreed or not. "We just… broke up. Take care of her," he said to her parents.

Mac ducked his head and walked by them, unable to meet their gazes.

"Mac," Amy said, hurrying to catch up with him.

She grabbed his forearm and gently stopped him.

"Give her time. I-I heard what you said. That you love her. Give her time. She's... *willful* and strong. Too strong, I think. All she's ever wanted to do is dance. I think she's lost without it."

He closed his hand over Amy's and gently squeezed. "I understand. But I can't stand by and watch her hurt herself."

"Her ex..." Amy rolled her eyes, shook her head. "He was all about appearances. He wouldn't have cared how much pain she had so long as she made him look good. Tonight? He would've had her in heels dragging her all over the city to show off. I can tell what you feel is real, Mac. And I'm sorry she hurt you. Just understand that she can't see the forest for the trees right now."

He acknowledged the woman's words with a nod. "I'm sorry, too. Good night, Amy. Vic."

Mac made his way out of the center and across the street to the parking garage. He climbed into his SUV and sat there a long moment before getting his phone and checking his texts, just in case.

Though there was a slew of questions from Marsali and one with a business question, there were none from V.

He stabbed the key into the ignition and gunned the engine, more than ready to get out of the suit and sit on his back deck.

He made it home in record time, the evening traffic light. In quick order, he poured a drink, stripped thanks to having not taken the laundry upstairs yet, and changed into sweats and a T-shirt before heading outside to— "What are you doing here?" he asked when he spotted Carter, Lincoln, and Oliver sitting on his back patio.

"We heard," Oliver stated simply. "Thought you could use some company."

"You should've stayed and enjoyed your dinner," Mac told them.

"Nah, we knew you'd be here licking your wounds," Carter said.

"The girls are there with Denz. He'll be sure they get home safely. We're more worried about you," Oliver continued.

"I'm good."

"Dude, you're so not good," Carter said. "And your shirt's on inside out."

Mac looked down to realize it was true and huffed out a laugh. "I guess it is." He thought about leaning forward and righting it but then shrugged. Why bother?

"What happened?" Lincoln asked.

Mac ran through the highlights of the evening post-dance, and all three of his buddies shook their heads.

"Stubborn."

"Maybe she'll come around."

"Crazy."

Mac glared at Carter, who shrugged.

"I don't mean *crazy* crazy, but crazy that she'd put long-term health over dancing for six months or a year."

"She'll see it eventually," Oliver said softly. "It may take her a while, but she'll see what she's doing eventually. I did."

"Not before Marsali dumped you," Mac said.

"Yeah, well, who's dumped now?" Oliver asked.

"It was mutual," Mac drawled, feeling as morose and down as a teenage boy dumped by his first girl. "But… I told her I love her."

A round of soft whistles and groans filled the air, adding to Mac's misery.

"So you told her," Oliver said. "Now you wait."

"If she gets an offer from New York, she'll be gone," Carter said.

"Pushing her won't do any good," Lincoln added. "She has to get there herself."

"Eliza said something similar," Mac told them. "One day at the dance studio. She said I had to let V decide whether to stay or go, but that I needed to make her never want to leave."

"Sounds like something she'd say," Carter said. "But did she say how or was it all in woman-speak no one really understands?"

"Obviously telling her I love her didn't work," he mused, staring into the depths of the glass he held. "So, no. I don't have a clue. But if she gets that call, Carter's right. She'll leave in a heartbeat."

IN THE WEE hours of the following morning just before dawn, V was bundled up and sitting on the condo's balcony overlooking the ocean when her phone bleeped.

She held the ice pack on her propped leg with one hand and picked the phone up before settling back in her seat with a barely suppressible groan.

Somehow she'd managed to walk out of the arts center two hours after her performance, but once in her father's truck, she'd asked her parents to take her to the emergency room.

Sure enough, a scan showed signs of hairline fractures around several of the pins in her leg. She had follow-up appointment cards in her purse for more scans, and in the hours since, the pain had barely lessened to a tolerable degree.

It had been a quiet ride back to the condo.

Now as she sat here, she faced the undeniable truth. It was over.

Dancing meant training. Hour after hour, day after day, week after week. It also meant performing after those hours of training had taken place only to get up and do it all again the next day.

Mac's words about thinking long-term came to mind, and she blinked back tears of truth she didn't want to acknowledge, much less accept. But having denied them all of this time, she knew she couldn't put it off any longer. He was right.

It was time to think ahead. Past time. Because her career as a professional dancer was over. Finished. As of last night.

"Honey, I made you a sandwich," her mother said from the open patio door. "Are you hungry? You need to eat something before you take those pain meds."

V shook her head, unable to speak due to the large lump in her throat making words impossible. The end brought too much loss to breathe. Too much sadness to speak.

"V? Oh, I didn't know you were on a call. Sorry."

Her mother set the plate down on the small table beside her, and V looked away so that her mother couldn't see the tears blinding her.

"I'll be back to check on you in a while," Amy said, entering the condo once more.

V held in her tears until her mother was gone and then glanced down at the phone in her hand, realizing the email had come from Jonathan Frakkes.

Apparently the man had finished writing his article in the airport and on the plane back to New York.

She took a breath in a poor attempt to slow her racing

heart as she clicked on the PDF file to read it through a sheen of tears.

While this journalist had planned to do a follow-up story on a broken ballerina, I find myself doing the opposite. Victoria Valentine has risen from the ashes like a phoenix, and her company will be lucky to get her back into the fold after the video of this performance goes viral as I know it will.

"Did it go viral?" she whispered, clicking out of the article long enough to get on social media. It wasn't hard to find.

Someone had taken the video from last night and split the screen, timing it with the first one. And this video had one point seven million views and counting. *In less than nine hours.*

V watched her performance, focusing on the one last night. In doing so, she spotted the moment the pain began to show itself, at least to her eyes. And even though she'd completed the intricate ballet like the professional she was, she found herself facing hard facts. She couldn't keep doing it. Not without endangering herself even more. She had to consider her quality of life.

"V? Is everything all right?" her mother asked from the doorway.

V held up the phone and swallowed hard. "The, um, article from Jonathan Frakkes. It hasn't even gone live yet, but someone posted video of me dancing. It's happening. It's gone viral like the other one."

V looked up to see her mother staring at her and obviously worried. "Stop. Okay? I get it. Finally. I'm sitting here staring at the ocean and forcing myself to accept that it's over, and I don't need I told you so's."

"Oh, honey, it wouldn't be like that."

"No?" V asked dryly. "I'm still glad I did it. Danced last night. I'm *glad* because at least this way I… I finished it and I *killed* it. Can you understand that? I had to know that I could."

"Yes. I-I understand," Amy said, her voice thick with tears as she moved to take the seat beside V.

"But what I don't know is how to start again."

"Honey—"

"I'm twenty-eight years old and I have to… Mom, I don't know how to *do* this," she said, voice cracking as she sniffled back the tears.

"V, no one said you can't dance again. Just not at the punishing level you have been. And tonight? Oh, baby, tonight proved just how amazing you are. You have that to keep and treasure for the rest of your life."

"But what now? I thought if I came here and I couldn't dance, I could at least take over Reels for Dad. But now I don't even have that to fall back on."

"Would you really have been happy bartending and managing the restaurant? Really—be honest," her mother said in a chiding tone. "How many times did you tell me how sick you were of drunks hitting on you?"

It was true. The restaurant was fun, the bar was great, but it wasn't something she pictured herself doing forever. "So what do I do? I don't want to go back to school, and I don't know how to work a regular job."

"Think about it. Think hard. I'm sure you'll come up with something, and just like tonight, no one will be able to stop you from accomplishing whatever you set your mind to."

"I suppose I could teach. I mean, working with the older kids made me remember what it was like to want to get out of regular classes and push myself, you know? To excel. Maybe the article… I could use it to get my foot in the door as a teacher."

"You would be wonderful at it," her mother said

without hesitation. "Just be sure it's what you really want if it could take you away. You have something pretty spectacular here."

"You mean Mac."

"Yeah, Mac. Honey, that man is head over heels for you."

"He…" She took a deep breath, filling her lungs with fresh salt air, trying and failing to ignore the pain. "He told me he loves me last night."

"I know."

She glanced at her mother and found Amy looking somewhat sheepish. Well, as sheepish as a nosy mother could.

"Your father and I were outside when… when you and Mac had words."

"You mean when he told me he loved me but I was stupid for following my dreams?"

Her mother chuckled. "Oh, I don't remember him using quite those words."

"Fine. Maybe not," V said begrudgingly, "but he did say he wouldn't stick around and watch me hurt myself."

"That more than anything should tell you how much he loves you."

"Mom… it's over."

"It's not over unless you want it to be. Sweetheart, could you really not tell how crazy he was at the sight of you in pain? The man was beside himself."

"But he doesn't understand that I'm not going to just give up."

"Oh, I think he sees that quite clearly. And isn't that just as important?"

"Really? You think you're qualified to give me relationship advice?" The words emerged before she could stop them, and V groaned long and loud. "I'm sorry. I'm sorry, Mom. That was uncalled for."

"Yes, it was. So here is some more truth for you since we're sharing it. You were too young to know anything about my relationship with your father when it ended. And Steve and I had a wonderful marriage until he died. But your father and I... That man has always held a special place in my heart."

"So why did you leave?"

"Because I had to. He's not the same man that he was back then, when he first got back from war. All I can say is that I'm thankful for whatever time we'll have together in the future because it allows me to know *this* man. The one I knew him to be before that changed him."

"I still don't get it. Why not stick it out?"

"Because I had a little girl to protect from a man who wouldn't seek counseling for the terrors that made him... He hurt me, Victoria. Oh, he didn't mean to, but he did. He'd... have a nightmare and strangle me and not even remember it the next day. I was terrified. For me and for you. When my family urged me to leave, I did. I had to. For us."

V felt like the ocean had come ashore, swallowed her, and she fought her way to the surface. "I had no idea. You never said anything."

"Because that man who had such horrible dreams wasn't the man I married. The man he is now. But it took a long time for him to return. He had to find his way back. Just like you have to find your way forward."

Find her way forward? "I don't know who I am if I'm not dancing. I've been in ballet since I was three."

"So? If you love it, continue. If you don't? Move on. The whole world is in front of you to do what you want. You have an advantage here in that no one is rushing you to figure things out, and you have the rest of your life ahead of you. That life can be whatever you choose to make it, whether you're dancing or not. Just choose."

V picked up the sandwich and ate, realizing suddenly that she was ravenous. She finished the sandwich and her mother held out the pain pill. V eyed it but knew if she was going to get any sleep she'd have to have help. She swallowed it back and ignored her mother's pleased look.

"Let me see that article," Amy said.

V handed over the phone and her mother read it aloud.

But whether it's dancing, teaching, or head of her own production, Victoria Valentine will return. This journalist guarantees it. You haven't seen the last of her yet.

"Well, there you go," Amy said, pleasure clouding her voice. "Now it's up to you to make it happen."

Chapter 27

Mac finished reading the article on Victoria's comeback and settled deeper into his seat at London's Lattes.

"Pretty cool, isn't it?" Marsali asked as she carried her order and joined him.

"Yeah. It's great."

She slid him a sisterly look and clasped her hands around her mug.

Mac felt Denz's gaze boring into his back when the man in the far corner of the coffeeshop stood and walked by Marsali to get another pastry.

The guys had stayed several hours and kept him company on the patio, drinking and talking and trying to cheer him up. It hadn't worked. And he reminded himself that he'd set himself up for this by agreeing to see V even after discovering her temporary status.

"So," Marsali said briskly. "It's my duty as a matchmaker to tell you that you have more matches left in our agreement."

"I'm not interested."

"I think you should be."

"I'm not, Marse. Not now."

"But maybe for me?"

Mac froze at the sound of V's voice and turned to find her on crutches, right leg in a brace.

"What the—" He jumped to his feet and offered her his chair, aware of Amy lifting a hand in greeting toward him from across the room. "Sit down. Are you all right?"

"Mac," Marsali said, eyes smiling, "I'd like you to meet your new match, Victoria D'Marco. Victoria, MacGregor Jones. And now that the introductions are in order, I'm going to visit with your mama," she said to V.

Marsali grabbed her purse and cup and quickly high-tailed it across the room to sit beside Amy at the bar, which, he noted, gave them a good view of the two of them. "Are you okay?" he asked when he moved to take Marsali's vacated chair.

"Yeah. I mean, I will be." She rolled her eyes and inhaled. "I would've called and had you meet me at the beach but... crutches... and then I wondered if you'd be willing to see me at all so... Please don't be mad at Marsali. I asked her to help."

"I'm not mad." Confused but not mad. "Frakkes's article was good."

"Yeah. My, uh, company called and asked me to return and take my old position back, and I've had other offers to dance and teach."

"So you came to say goodbye?" He really didn't need her to do that. Not when it had ripped his heart out to walk away from the dressing room.

"Not exactly."

He waited, and seconds ticked by with her looking more uncomfortable by the— "D'Marco?"

A smile pulled her lips up at the corners.

"I wondered when you were going to pick up on that."

"I don't understand." What did using her legal name mean?

"I, um, started thinking about what you said while I was in the hospital getting checked out. It took me a while, but I realized if you were the one doing something that hurt you, *I'd* be upset if you kept doing it. I had no right to be so... I'm sorry."

"Apology accepted. How's the leg?"

"I... might have stress fractures. I have to wait for someone to read the scans, but it looks that way. Either way, I have pain when I dance. More than I should, and more than I wanted to admit to. You were right. I have to think of my health and future, and I have to come up with a new plan."

Mac watched her as she spoke, and he stretched his hands across the table to hold hers, enveloping her palms in his.

"Mac, I don't know what the future holds for me, but it's not dancing professionally. I realize that now. I... accept it. But that performance—I needed that. I finished what I'd started and I did it well, and I'm okay with... going out on top, as they say. Teaching is definitely an option and one I'm drawn to. I have a place in mind but..."

The way she worded her statement left him struggling to draw breath. "Where?"

"Here. In Wilmington. But you were so upset with me I wasn't sure if you'd want me to stay or for us to see each other after...? I mean, that's why I contacted Marsali and she... I-I thought if you would agree to date the new me—the non-dancing Victoria D'Marco, who isn't sure what the next career move is going to be— maybe we could start over and get to know each other and..."

Mac stood so fast his chair scraped against the wood

floor in a noisy announcement of his intentions as he leaned over the small table and kissed her.

V laughed against his lips, and he heard a few claps and whistles as he somehow managed to get around the table without lifting his mouth from hers.

"Mmftm… wait. Is that a yes?" she asked.

She smiled up at him with those striking blue eyes of hers, and he took her mouth again, this kiss longer, sweeter, slower, more revealing than any before. "It's definitely a yes."

From across the room, he heard Amy and Marsali giggling.

"I love romance, don't you?" Marsali asked.

Mac ignored his gushing, romance-loving sister and tilted V's chair back onto two legs, holding it while she laughed and gripped his arms for balance. "Victoria D'Marco."

"Yes?"

"I want to date you, and I support you. Dancer, teacher, or whatever you decide to be."

Her smile fell and her eyes filled with tears she didn't try to hide. She slid one palm up his arm to stroke his face, her fingertips lightly touching his mouth.

"MacGregor Jones, I love you, too."

V COULDN'T HAVE IMAGINED Oliver and Marsali's fall wedding. She simply didn't have the vision. But apparently Eliza had, and when a matchmaker and a Hollywood star got hitched and the bride's best friend was a wedding planner married to a contractor, things got done. Big-time.

When Marsali had announced the venue to be the Live Oaks at Ft. Fisher, Mac had taken V there, and V had guessed things would be prettied up in typical wedding fashion.

Oh, no.

The majestic trees became a glowing backdrop, gnarled branches draped with tulle and floating candles, with a wooden board swing with thick rope wound with fairy lights that now glittered and flickered in the growing dusk as the sun showed its final colors.

The ceremony had been timed perfectly, the glorious sky blasting out shades of burgundy and purple that couldn't have been planned ahead, but an answer in response to the prayers for the day.

Guests oohed and ahhed and wiped away tears due to the beauty of the moment and the undeniable love the bride and groom shared as they made their lives one.

But as the sun set and the noise of press-owned drones faded away, the backdrop really came alive. It turned into a magical fairyland complete with a small trickling fountain Carter and his crew had set up at the center of the action. Guests were favored with flexible lights at the end of long wands, and when waved, they looked like dancing fireflies.

V smiled as Piper danced and twirled her way across the wooden dance floor. She often heard how the little girl wanted to be a mermaid, but Piper showed promise in ballet. Time would tell if it was a passing fancy.

She rubbed her hands up and down her arms to ward off the early October chill beginning to set in and found herself wrapped in the gorgeous scarf Marsali had gifted the bridesmaids with and the loving arms of her man.

"What has you looking so pensive?"

"Mmm, not pensive," she said, smiling up at Mac. "Just… taking it all in."

"Ah, that's right. You haven't seen Eliza work her magic before. I forgot."

"This is—"

"Completely over-the-top but perfect for the bride and groom? Yeah. She has that gift."

"It's amazing. I mean… *amazing*."

He squeezed her gently and his warmth and strength sent a chill down her body as he cuddled her close.

"How's the leg?"

"It's fine. Stop worrying." Her dance at the recital had in fact caused three hairline fractures at various points. Thankfully they hadn't required surgery.

"Not worry where you're concerned? I don't think that's possible, woman. Not with your stunts."

She smiled and shook her head but knew why he said that. She'd remained on the crutches, leg in a brace, for eight weeks, and then went back to physical therapy for a grueling twelve weeks. And even though she was supposed to be resting, she'd managed a few trips up the stairs and the like at various times.

During the last month, she and Mrs. Taylor had reached an agreement in regard to the studio and V's desire to purchase it versus start afresh as Mrs. Taylor's competition.

She and Mac had toured various areas throughout Wilmington and the island searching for the perfect location to house a dance studio, but something drew her back to Mrs. Taylor's time and again, and V had finally worked up the nerve to approach the woman.

Offers had poured in after her performance in April, both to dance and to teach, and she'd forced herself to go through the process of virtual interviews regarding the teaching positions, just to learn her worth as such.

They were willing to wait for her to recover from the setback, but V hadn't kept them waiting and turned down the offers after noting the various others to teach.

While she'd loved working under Mrs. Taylor, it was time for her to step into her future, rather than ride along on someone else's. So while her body healed, she and Mac had begun the process of seeking out a location for V to open a dance studio.

With a carefully crafted business plan, V realized so long as people continued to have children, there would be little girls and boys who wanted to dance. Thank God. It was an art form that needed to be cherished, a beautiful gift that had played out for centuries and would for many more.

Now, a month had passed since she'd been finally released from PT, and she could no longer put off her future. It was decision time.

"Something's up with you," Mac murmured. "You're too quiet. What's going on in that beautiful head of yours?"

V turned in his arms and lifted her face to better see him.

She needed to be here in Carolina Cove. Wanted to be here. Closer to Mac and her parents, her friends… Oh, her new friends had welcomed her with open arms—another vast difference from the competitive dance crowd.

Instead of backstabbing and always fighting to get a leg up, her friends were strong and beautiful, funny and supportive, and she'd be crazy to not see it. Crazier still to give up a man who looked at her like he did right now. "Dance with me?"

He dropped a kiss on her forehead. "I thought you'd never ask."

Mac took her hand and led the way to the dance floor, drew her into his arms. She welcomed the heat of him as he pulled her close. "I have a surprise for you," she whispered.

"When do I get it?"

"Later."

He lifted his head and gave her an ornery grin full of hope, and she laughed softly at his expression. "Down, boy."

Mac kissed her temple and shrugged. "You know me well. I have a surprise for you, too."

She stared at him and slowly dipped her fingers into her cleavage—what little there was of it—and pulled the ribboned key she'd tucked there earlier.

"Well, you've got my attention," Mac said in his oh-so-sexy Carolinian drawl.

"This is for you—but you can't keep it. At least not yet."

Mac shifted his hand to hold hers and seemingly ponder the key in question.

"If that's to your father's condo, I doubt he'd want me to have it," he said.

"It's not—it's a key… to my future."

Mac stopped swaying and stared down at her with an expression that tore her heart to shreds and put it back together again. He was afraid to hope but he was and that? That confirmed what she already knew. This man loved her. Really loved her.

"Come again?"

"We've been looking all over Wilmington for the perfect place for a studio when it's been here on the island the entire time. Mrs. Taylor is retiring and you," she said, "are looking at the new owner of the dance studio."

"The new… Seriously? You bought it? Why didn't you say anything? I could've helped you with the—"

"Because I wanted to do it myself. And… *bought* is a malleable word. Mrs. Taylor and I came to an agreement, which Vic helped me research thoroughly, and we came to terms Vic advised as agreeable. And, yes, there were attorneys involved. Anyway, I took over her lease and will be paying her a percentage of fees for a set period of time to purchase the dance side of the business and the contracts she has with her students and parents."

Mac's hands shifted to her face and held her while he lowered his head. He kissed her, every ounce of happiness he felt reflected in the embrace.

V gripped his arms for balance and reveled in the kiss, knowing without a doubt she'd made the right decision. The night couldn't get any more magical than this.

Mac ended the kiss and hugged her close.

"Before you freak out, I have permission from the bride."

Permission from the bride? V frowned at his words before Mac straightened and took a knee in front of her. V gasped at the sight of him, glancing around quickly because of the stir it created with the guests, only to look back to see him pulling an utterly gorgeous ring from a velvet box.

"Oh! It's happening!" Marsali cried from somewhere nearby.

Mac looked a little sheepish at the scene, and she loved him all the more for setting aside ego and pride and giving her the romance.

"Victoria D'Marco, I love you. And I can't imagine my future without you. Would you do me the honor of becoming my bride?"

V nodded, eyes flooded with tears, and finally managed to whisper a soft yes.

Mac slid the ring onto her trembling hand and rose, sweeping her up into his arms for a kiss that promised the future and more.

Cheers went up among the crowd, and when things calmed down, Oliver and Marsali offered a toast to them.

The music began playing again, and people congratulated them as they returned to the dance floor.

Marsali, Eliza, Amelia, and Izzy surrounded her to check out the ring before Mac firmly extracted her and pulled her into his arms to dance.

"Mac," Marsali said, her tone teasing, "I expect a glowing review now that you've found your eighth."

Mac's chuckles filled her ears, and V pressed her cheek to his solid chest and smiled at her future sister-in-law.

She'd thought she'd regret joining Marsali's database, but given the results, there just weren't enough stars.

"I have one more surprise for you," Mac whispered.

She frowned, really hoping he wasn't about to spring a surprise wedding, because she wanted one of her own. "Oh?"

"All you need to do is focus on paying off Mrs. Taylor. Don't worry about the lease."

"What? Why do you say that?"

He chuckled as he tucked her close and dipped her, stealing a kiss.

"Because you'll own a fourth of the building very soon."

I HOPE YOU ENJOYED READING PERFECTLY MISMATCHED! KEEP READING BELOW FOR A SNEAK PEEK AT BY THE BOOK!

EXCERPT: Almost six hours later, they crossed the Snow's Cut Bridge and kept going to Carolina Cove.

During the long drive, she'd made a mental list of fun things to do that Tommy might like.

She thought they could take the top and doors off the Jeep and drive out on the beach to fish. Go visit the *USS North Carolina* battleship moored in downtown Wilmington.

Rent Jet Skis. Maybe take the ferry to Bald Head Island and get a golf cart for the day to explore?

Anything that might possibly reverse the sour frown permanently marring her son's face of late.

She made the turns leading to her parents' home and pulled into the drive, ready for a long stretch and walk on the beach to clear her head and help her figure out a plan for the future now that she was jobless.

She had a small savings and a severance package, which would help cover expenses short-term, but finding a new job was paramount. "Hey," she said to Tommy. "I'm sure Grandpa's *really* missed you, so don't be rolling your eyes or giving him attitude. Got it?"

"Whatever."

She fought her urge to roll her own eyes at her son's mood and got out of the Wrangler, noting the strange vehicle in the driveway. "Let's take a load up to the apartment as we go," she ordered, opening the rear door to hand off bags to her grumpy son.

She found the right key before loading up and making her way to the stairs beside the garage. "Tommy? Are you coming?"

"Get the door open first," Tommy said with a grumble. "There's nowhere to stand up there."

The landing at the top of the stairs *was* narrow, but she doubted that was his reasoning. Lately Tommy was dead set against anything he deemed she wanted. Blue was green, wrong was right, and nothing made him happy. But how much of it was typical teen hormones and how much of it mourning for his father?

Sweating, huffing, and straining beneath the weight of the multiple bags she carried, she dropped what was in her right hand and removed the key ring she'd held in her mouth for the trudge up the stairs.

She tried the key but it didn't fit—maybe because the lock looked brand-new?

Salt air did a lot of damage to such things, so it was little surprise that it had needed to be changed since their last trip two years ago. Still—

The door opened with a yank, and she stepped back, unbalanced by the bags and the surprise of the half-naked man on the other side. A man who quickly reached out and grabbed her by the shoulders to keep her from tumbling backward over the railing, weighted down by luggage.

She blinked, eyes flaring when she took in his wet skin, the damp towel around his slim and tightly honed waist, and a muscle-ripped chest that would've looked like something out of *GQ* if not for the bruises and scars.

Was that a *gunshot* wound?

Scott had had one from his first tour, and the two looked the same.

"Can I help you?"

"Uh…"

The man raised an eyebrow and released his grip on her shoulders, a pained expression flashing over his features as he lowered his injured arm.

"You hurt yourself grabbing me," she said, her gazing shifting to his shoulder to keep from looking into brown eyes that seemed to bore into her soul.

"It's fine."

"Mom, come on. What's the deal?" Tommy called from below.

The man crossed his arms over his chest, but she noted it was probably more to cradle and relieve the pain of his injured arm. "Uh, I'm not sure," she said, shifting her gaze to the man once again. Considering he stood there in nothing but a towel, it was hard to focus. "I'm Claire Simmons. My father owns the house and... Who are you?"

"Marcus Denz," he said. "I'm his renter."

"Claire?" her father called from the bottom of the stairs. "What are you doing here?"

KEEP READING BY THE BOOK.

MAKE ME A MATCH SERIES:

- ROMANCE RESET
- RULES OF ENGAGEMENT
- THE MATCHMAKER'S SECRET
- PERFECTLY MISMATCHED
- BY THE BOOK

MONTANA SECRETS SERIES:

- HEALING HER COWBOY
- IT HAD TO BE YOU
- HERS TO KEEP
- MILLION DOLLAR STANDOFF
- HIS CHRISTMAS WISH
- THEIR SECRET SON

THE SEASIDE SISTERS SERIES:

- THE LAST GOODBYE
- LATTES AND LULLABYES
- MAP OF DREAMS
- WORTH THE RISK
- LOST LOVE FOUND

TAMING THE TULANES SERIES:

- SMALL TOWN SCANDAL
- THEIR SECRET BARGAIN
- CROSSING THE LINE
- THE NANNY'S SECRET
- SOMEONE TO TRUST

THE STONE RIVER SERIES:

- WORTH THE WAIT
- NOT BY SIGHT
- THROUGH THE VALLEY

- LEAD ME NOT
- CHRISTMAS AT HOLLY WOOD
- THEIR CHRISTMAS MIRACLE
- SECOND CHANCES

SMALL TOWN SCANDALS SERIES:

- BRODY'S REDEMPTION
- FALLING FOR HER BOSS
- WITH THIS MAN

SECRET SANTA SERIES:

- SECRET SANTA
- SECRET SANTA II: A CHRISTMAS TO REMEMBER

MAKE ME A MATCH SERIES:

- ROMANCE RESET
- RULES OF ENGAGEMENT
- THE MATCHMAKER'S SECRET
- PERFECTLY MISMATCHED
- BY THE BOOK

FAQ

Is Carolina Cove a real place?

Carolina Cove is purely fictional; however, it is *loosely* based on one of my favorite places—Kure Beach, North Carolina. Kure Beach is home to a wonderful pier, a pavilion for special events like weddings and birthdays, swings facing the Atlantic, pelicans Pete and George, coffee shops, restaurants, and more. It's also close to the North Carolina Aquarium, Carolina Beach, and Wilmington.

Can I stay at the Carolina Cove Inn?

While Carolina Cove and the Carolina Cove Inn are purely fictional, there are plenty of motels and rentals in the area to enjoy.

But the pier is real?

Yes! And it has quite a history. Be sure to check out the Kure Beach Pier Cam for a view of Kure Beach and the Atlantic.

What about the restaurants and coffee shops and places you've mentioned in the series?

London's Lattes is based on two of my favorite local coffee shops in Kure Beach and Carolina Beach. Are there more? Yes, plenty. But those two shops I know well because I've visited fairly often while writing these stories. Neither of them on their own was perfect for what I had in mind for London's, however, so I basically combined the two and ta-da! London's Lattes was born. But, no, if you go into either of them, you won't find London's exact business. Isn't fiction wonderful?

Why make up a city? Why not use Kure Beach?

One of the best things about writing fiction is that when a story appears a certain way, you can write it just that way. Carolina Cove and the characters appeared to me in story form and while Kure Beach IS one of my favorite places, I had to change some things to better fit the series as well as steer far away from any real-life persons/families for obvious reasons. Doing so, that meant also changing the name of the city, etc. But, that said, you will find a slew of similarities in the fictional city and the real one. :)

Where is the dream catcher mailbox?

Unfortunately the dream catcher mailbox is pure fiction and an idea taken from a "beach mailbox" I visited once many years ago. The dream catcher mailbox first appeared in the SEASIDE SISTERS SERIES.

How did you research the matchmaking aspect?

Oh, the answer to this was fun! Wilmington actually has a professional matchmaker. I interviewed her to get my details straight and learned a lot about a very fascinating business!

MAKE ME A MATCH SERIES:

- ROMANCE RESET
- RULES OF ENGAGEMENT
- THE MATCHMAKER'S SECRET
- PERFECTLY MISMATCHED
- BY THE BOOK

About the Author

Kay Lyons always wanted to be a writer, ever since the age of seven or eight when she copied the pictures out of a Charlie Brown book and rewrote the story because she didn't like the plot. Through the years her stories have changed but one characteristic stayed true— they were all romances. Each and every one of her manuscripts included a love story.

Published in 2005 with Harlequin Enterprises, Kay's first release was a national bestseller. Kay has also been a HOLT Medallion, Book Buyers Best and RITA Award nominee. Look for her most recent novels with Kindred Spirits Publishing.

For more information regarding her work, please visit Kay at the following:

www.kaylyonsauthor.com

@KayLyonsAuthor (Twitter)

Kay Lyons Author (Facebook)

Author_Kay_Lyons (Instagram)

Kay Lyons, Author (Pinterest)

SIGN UP FOR KAY'S NEWSLETTER AND RECEIVE UPDATES ON NEW RELEASES, CONTESTS, PRE-RELEASE BOOK INFORMATION, EXCLUSIVES AND MORE!

9 781953 375049